THE BATTLE OF BUCKEYE ESTATES

BY JASON C. HOBBINS

Cover layout and design by Eliza McCartney

DEDICATION

This book is dedicated to my son, whose nickname is "Bird". There isn't a day that goes by that I don't teach him something, and he, in turn, instructs me

Table Of Contents

CAST OF CHARACTERS
WEST ESTATES

Timothy "Little Timmy" Lyle 5th Grade
Mary Margaret "Maggie" Lyle 7th Grade
Bode Wayne Catron 7th Grade
Brooklyn "Brook" Catron 4th Grade
Samantha Peckenpaugh 7th Grade
Steven Peckenpaugh 8th Grade
Sara Peckenpaugh 5th Grade
Shaun Peckenpaugh 3rd Grade
Marc Powell 7th Grade
Cortney "Rosie" Rosenberry 8th Grade
Cree Taylor 4th Grade
Jesse "Big Jesse" Taylor 7th Grade

CAST OF CHARACTERS
EAST ESTATES

Maci Childress 8th Grade
Darin "Sneak" Coleman 7th Grade
Gregory Hammond 7th Grade
Jared Hanson 7th Grade
Melissa "Missy" Hanson 4th Grade
Lexi Riggs 8th Grade
Blake Riggs 7th Grade
Joy Shaw 8th Grade
Kelsey Shaw 7th Grade
David "Dorkboy" Boerner 7th Grade

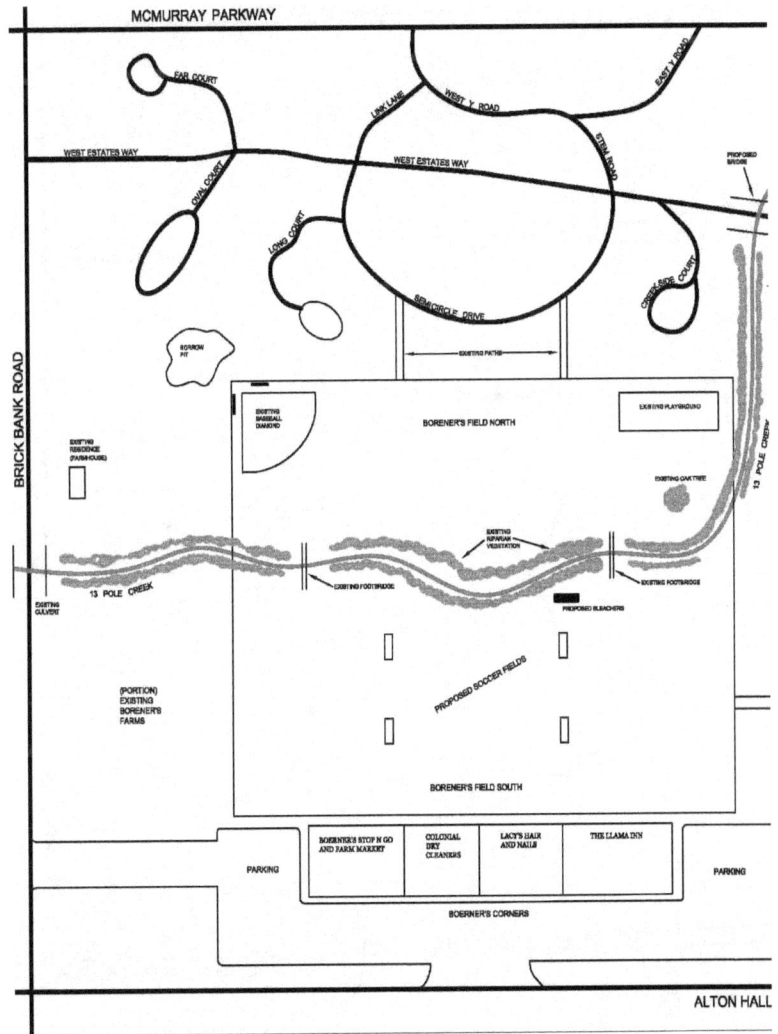

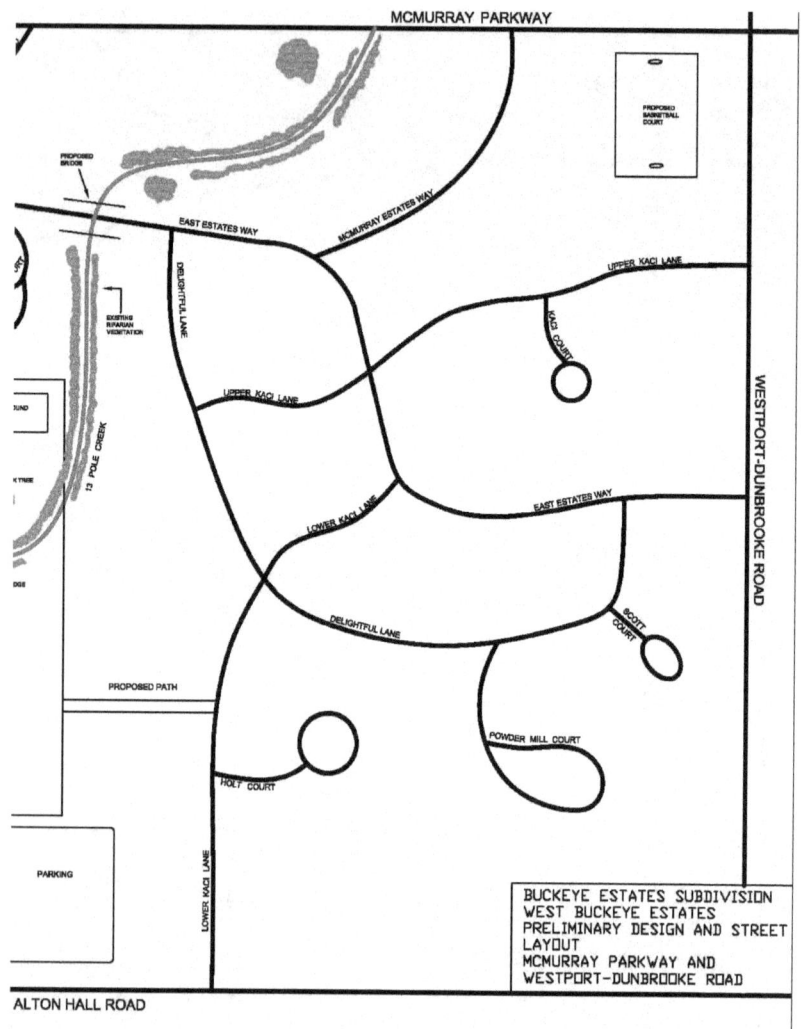

MCMURRAY PARKWAY

PROPOSED
BASKETBALL
COURT

PROPOSED
BRIDGE

EAST ESTATES WAY

MCMURRAY ESTATES WAY

UPPER KACI LANE

EXISTING
RIPARIAN
VEGETATION

DELIGHTFUL LANE

KACI COURT

WESTPORT-DUNBROOKE ROAD

UPPER KACI LANE

13 POLE CREEK

LOWER KACI LANE

EAST ESTATES WAY

DELIGHTFUL LANE

SCOTT COURT

PROPOSED PATH

POWDER MILL COURT

HOLT COURT

PARKING

LOWER KACI LANE

BUCKEYE ESTATES SUBDIVISION
WEST BUCKEYE ESTATES
PRELIMINARY DESIGN AND STREET
LAYOUT
MCMURRAY PARKWAY AND
WESTPORT-DUNBROOKE ROAD

ALTON HALL ROAD

CHAPTER 1
LAST DAY OF SCHOOL

It was just after lunch on the last day of school at Prairie View Middle School. The promise of summer break had every kid in the school amped up and ready to go. Summer to them meant sleeping in, hanging out at the West Plains pool, vacations or just plain doing nothing all day. Summer meant hot sunny days, t-shirts and shorts, flip-flops and sandals, ice cream and sweat.

It had been a harsh winter and spring for Central Ohio, which made this summer even more anticipated, welcomed and wanted. Everyone had their share of shoveling snow, stuck cars, dirty slush and in February, temperatures that didn't get out of the single digits. When spring came, it brought rain with it. A lot of rain! Basements were flooded, roads became small rivers and fields became mud pits. Now, summer was here and all of that was behind them. It was going to be a great summer.

Bode Catron and his best friend, "Big" Jessie Taylor walked down the hall to their next class. Even though they both loathed math class, it didn't matter at this point. Testing was done and the teacher would probably have them play a couple of cheesy math games and call it a day.

"So, are you gonna play any other position besides catcher," Bode smirked at Big Jessie.

"Man, when you're the best at something, why switch," Big Jessie shot back a confident smirk of his own.

Jared Hanson and his best friend, Blake Riggs were walking in the opposite direction towards the last English class of the year. It was no problem because the teacher would have them study by themselves while he worked on other things or pretended not to be asleep. Not only were they excited about summer break and vacations in general, but especially about soccer games on south field. In addition, Jared, Blake and most of their friends were also enrolled in the Kickstart Summer Soccer Camp held at the local high school each year.

Bode and Jared's eyes met as they approached each other. The jovial mood of just a few seconds ago faded quickly. Both were now glaring at each other, eyes locked for the entire three seconds it took to pass. The reality now came flooding back to them of the divided nature of the subdivision they both called home.

"Man, I can't stand that guy," Jared said after they passed.

"I can't stand any of them," Blake hissed.

Bode and Big Jessie had the same sentiments.

Bode spoke first. "Dude better quit staring man," he said, punching the palm of his hand "or were gonna have a reenactment of last spring," referring to a playground fight he and Jared had just before school ended in 6th grade.

"They don't know who they're messing with," Big Jessie added.

That afternoon Lexi Riggs, Blake's sister, and her best friend, Maci Childress were out waiting for the bus when Maggie Lyle walked by.

"Oh, look out, its anger management girl," Lexi whispered. Maci snickered. Maggie didn't hear what was said, but heard the whisper. Always quick to anger, she whirled around to confront them.

"Got a problem, because I'm ready for one," Maggie said, hands on her hips in a defiant stance. Maci smirked and crossed her arms, looking at her. Lexi waved Maggie off with her hand, a disgusted look on her face. Maggie continued to stare at them, arms outstretched as she walked backward to her bus.

It was going to be a great summer.

CHAPTER 2
THE MAKINGS OF A RIVELRY

The kids of Buckeye Estates were always at war in a sense. A dislike has been around since the neighborhood was finished several years ago. Most of the kids from the west didn't like the kids from the east and visa versa. The west felt that they were there first, and the kids of the east were outsiders, intruding on their playgrounds and Boerner's field. They simply referred to the kids of the east as "Others" meaning they were unimportant.

Before it was built, East Estates was a large stand of woods that the kids from the west would play in. They made paths through the woods and would ride their bikes on them, lie in wait in them and scare other kids, play war and just generally hang out. It was their retreat from parents and the outside world. Now all of that was gone and replaced with homes and streets with names like Delightful Lane, which the west thought was stupid.

When the builders designed the east half, they made slightly bigger streets, lots and slightly bigger homes than those of the west. The kids of the west thought that since the east had bigger homes and backyards, they had a lot of money which really wasn't true. They also thought that if people had money, there were automatically snotty. The kids of the east felt this dislike and developed an attitude of their own. If they didn't like them because of what they had or thought they had, fine. They felt they had just as much right to play in Boerner's Field as the west did. That's just the way it was.

Boerner's field was a long, oval field. It was nestled right up next to Buckeye Estates. The Boerner Family, who were local farmers, owned a lot of the land near the subdivision and sold some of it for use as a park and play area, hence the locals called it Boerner's field. Various paths connected the field to the two halves of the subdivision. A creek ran east and west, cutting through the large field before running north, dividing the field as well as Buckeye Estates. Although its official name is Thirteen Pole Creek, everyone knew it as the "Divide".

The north portion of the field had a baseball diamond and playground. The south portion of the field had a soccer field and a playground. Bridges in two locations connect the north and south fields across the "Divide". To the south of Boerner field is a strip mall with four businesses in it, Boerner's Stop 'N' Go and Farm Market, Colonial Dry Cleaners and Laundromat, Laci's Hair and Nails and a restaurant, The Llama Inn. Boerner's Stop 'N' Go and Farm Market was very popular with the kids as they could stock up on candy, pop and ice cream. To the west of Boerner's field, was the Boerner Farm, which, to the kids of Buckeye Estates, stretched for miles, possibly in their minds to the next state. To the kids of Buckeye Estates, the field was the epicenter of the entire neighborhood.

Both sides did have an unspoken agreement for the most part. The kids of the west stayed in the north field and played baseball; the kids of the east stayed in the south field and played soccer. In a way, the west controlled the north field; the "Others" commanded the south.

Occasionally, some kids from the east would play baseball in the north field or someone from the west would wander down to the south field to play soccer, but it was a rare occasion. When these occurrences did happen, the intruders were met with muffled whispers and mean stares. Sometimes a home run would be hit and land near the soccer fields. The baseball would then be flung back over the divide, accompanied with shouts of "what are you trying to do, kill someone?" or "watch what you're doing!" Nobody in the past was ever hit or hurt by a fly ball and nothing serious resulted from the intrusions.

CHAPTER 3
THE PLAYGROUND THREE

Brooklyn "Brook" Catron, Cree Taylor and Melissa "Missy" Hanson were inseparable. The three would spend hours, even days on the North Field playground. They were in the same 4st grade class at Prairie View Elementary, and played together at recess, sat together at lunch and did their homework together. One was rarely seen without the other two. Their favorite thing to do is play on the North Field Playground and listen to Colin Searcy, a local pop singer who made it big on You Tube and was now an international sensation. All day long in the summer they would swing and sing Colin's songs at the top of their lungs. They would all sing in unison "Baby, you know I'm here for you, Baby, you know it's just me and you". It earned them the nickname "The Playground Three".

Missy heard her name called. She was at the North Field playground with Brook and Cree as usual. It was the first day of summer vacation.

"I gotta go, Mom and I are going shopping at the Mall and I'm gonna try to get her to buy it for me for my birthday," Missy said enthusiastically referring to Colin Searcy's new five disc boxset with B sides and unreleased material and a DVD.

"Do you think she will," Cree asked, almost jumping out of her skin.

"I hope so," she replied, "but I doubt it, she says money's tight right now and it's expensive."

"I tried to get my mom to download it, but she said no, she wasn't going to pay for it," Cree chimed in.

"Oh, I can't wait, I can't wait, I can't wait to own it," Brook shouted.

"Okay, I gotta go, see you tomorrow," Missy said as she crossed the bridge across the divide, her MP3 player and speakers in a brown case tucked under her arm.

All three girls smiled, waved and went their separate ways. Brook and Cree headed to West Estates and Missy to the East. As Brook and Cree walked passed the ball field on the way home, Brook eyed a baseball glove lying on the ground. She picked it up and looked at it. Scrawled in permanent marker on the inside pocket was the name "Bode C."

"Oh, that's my brother's," she thought to herself and took it home with her where she casually tossed it on a shelf in the garage.

CHAPTER 4
BODE AND JARED

Brook and Cree were technically from the west and Missy from the east, but none cared. They were great friends and too busy playing and talking to care about the politics of the older kids. Unfortunately, their older brothers didn't feel the same way.

Bode Catron despised the "Others" of the east. They thought they were snobs who looked down on the West. They also acted like they owned the soccer fields of South field. Bode was a big kid for 7th grade, stocky with blonde hair, blue eyes and ruddy cheeks. He always wore football, hockey or baseball jerseys because of his size, despite the weather. He would play any sport that he could, whenever he could. Bode was also a hothead and very quick to anger. If the west had a leader, it was Bode. He was a natural leader. It was also safe to say that he had no love for Jared.

"Big" Jessie Taylor was Bode's best friend and right-hand man. He was not as tall as Bode, but was built like a tank; his dark skin was a contrast to his light brown eyes.

He sported an afro style hair-do saying it was a way to pay homage to his heritage. "Big" Jessie was a lot calmer than Bode, but still had no love loss for the other of the East. The two were excellent baseball players and would practice batting, throwing and fielding whenever they could.

Missy's older brother, Jared, was sick of the way the kids of the west would stare at him and his friends when they played soccer, whispering and pointing. What was worse, he and some others from East Estates would try to play baseball on the north field ball diamond more than a few times and were met with an attitude. The west always said the game was full when Jared and the others could clearly see that they didn't have enough players to field two teams.

Jared was very athletic with a slender, in shape build, curly brown hair and dimples. He was a good looking kid, and that was another reason Bode despised him. All the girls gravitated toward him and it made Bode sick, and secretly jealous. It didn't help that it was well known that the one girl Bode liked was also enamored with Jared, Samantha Peckenpaugh.

It had been rumored that Samantha was the reason they fought on the playground last spring just before school ended.

Jared always thought Bode was stuck up and thought he was better than everyone else, which really wasn't true, but Jared made himself believe this. Jared was secretly jealous of Bode because, despite his size, could play every sport he tried. Jared had always wanted to play football, but was never considered because of his slender build where Bode always made the team as a linebacker.

Blake Riggs was Jared's best friend and right-hand man. Blake was a slender kid with all-American good looks and short brown, styled hair. He was very athletic and shared Jared's love of all sports, no matter what the sport was. He also shared Jared's contempt for the west. He had been there when the west turned them away from baseball games on North Field or basketball games at nearby Buckeye Park.

CHAPTER 5
BARTON ROAD CREAM SODA

Three freshman boys from nearby Westmont High School wandered into Boerner's Stop 'N' Go. They heard that Boerner's was the only store around that carried the new Barton Road Cream Soda. Since every other pop or soda that BR made was awesome, they were anxious to try it. They each grabbed a bottle, paid for it and out the door they went. Once outside, they all quickly opened their cream sodas and took big long slugs.

"Yuck," one said

"Tastes like some kinda nasty cough syrup," said another with a huge scowl on his face.

The third boy spit his out on the second try. "Gross man," was all he could say.

"Let me try again" the first boy said and took another long swig.

"This sucks."

"Maybe it's just a bad batch, spoiled or something."

"I don't know, but I'm taking mine back."

The other two agreed and back to Boerner's they went to plead their case. However, it was not in their favor. Jim Boerner, one of the Boerner boys was a nice kid who worked at his father's store. Jim was very forgiving when it came to younger kids but with high schoolers, he always thought that they were trying to get away with something.

"Sorry guys," Jim said, "I can't give you your money back on those,"

"Why not," the three boys protested.

"Well, you drank most of it for one".

"But it's a bad batch or something" one of them protested, "We just want to exchange them for something else."

"Sorry guys, you guys know the unique flavors BR has, plus you only have a drink left, just down it and don't get it again" Jim was persistent, waiting for the situation to get tense as he leaned over the counter.

The three finally gave up, threw out what was left, and took their loss. One of them, however, was a little more ticked off than the other two. That night, in a fit of childish revenge, he took a can of spray paint, crept up to the side of Boerner's when the coast was clear, and scrawled on the wall in big huge letters for all to see:

"BR SUCKS AND SO DO YOU GET RID OF THEM ALL."

The next day, as the east was gearing up for a soccer game, Greg returned from Boerner's with a sports drink.

"Anyone see what was painted on the side of Boerner's."

A lot of kids asked what was written so he repeated what was painted on the wall. Jared stopped putting on his cleats and looked at Greg with an inquisitive look, than to Blake. Blake looked at him with a piercing glare.

"You think that means you, your initials I mean"? Jared asked.

"They are probably just talking about Barton Road Cola, not you, Blake, It's no big............"

"Oh, they're talking about me," Blake cut Joy's words off in mid sentence with a stern look.

"I'm with you," Jared said, agreeing.

Blake continued "and I know exactly who wrote it".

"So super dramatic," Joy said, shaking her head.

CHAPTER 6
COLLISION AT THE SKATE PARK

The skate park off of McMurray Parkway was awesome. It had three bowls and several walls and jumps that skaters could hone their skills, talk to other skaters, and mess themselves up pretty good. It also had a couple of blind corners that skaters could run into each other pretty easily. The unspoken rule was to yell as you were approaching a blind spot, and hopefully avoid a collision. This didn't happen right after summer break with Blake and Mark Powell. Blake was barreling down an incline on his skateboard when Mark shot out in front of him. They collided which sent them both reeling. They were ok, but that didn't stop them from pointing fingers.

"Man, watch it, Dude," Blake was the first to speak up.

"Me??? Why didn't you yell or something?" Mark retorted.

"I did, open your ears, man," Blake responded, picking himself off of the concrete.

"Then you need to get the junk out of your mouth cause I didn't hear you," Mark picked up his skateboard and was walking toward Blake at this point. Other kids started to surround them, the situation getting uglier by the second.

"Well get the junk out of your ears," was all Blake could get out as Mark surged toward him. Blake did the same but both were quickly stopped by a group of kids, holding them both back.

"This ain't the end of this, Riggs," Mark blurted out as he was being led away by Big Jessie, Steven and a few other kids.

"Bring it," Blake yelled as he was dragged back by the Hammond boys.

CHAPTER 7
IN ENEMY TERRITORY

Not all kids were concerned about a rivalry; in fact, some could have cared less such as Rosie, Joy and Kelsey.

Cortney Rosenberry, whom everyone called Rosie, and Joy Shaw, an "Other", were best friends. Cortney was a tall, strongly built girl with a head of cascading curly, dark blonde hair. Her dad always said that if she were to wear a blue and white checkerboard skirt and knee high socks she would belong somewhere in a rolling meadow in Switzerland.

Joy, on the other hand, was a short, thin, wisp of a girl with a spattering of freckles, blue eyes, high cheek bones and long sandy blonde hair. Both girls didn't care that they were supposed to not like each other and thought the whole thing was stupid. They were in the same 8th grade class. They had known each other since kindergarten. They read the same books, liked the same music and had the same "live and let live" attitude.

Both girls realized that disliking someone for nothing was too much work. The only thing that they didn't have in common was sports. Rosie had no interest in sports and Joy was a fierce competitor, especially on the soccer field. She was one of the most feared, and one of the most sought-after soccer players on South Field, as well as other two organized leagues she played in. Everyone wanted Joy on their team.

Joy's younger sister, Kelsey was actually taller than her older sister by an inch. In fact the only thing that made them look like sisters was Kelsey had freckles and high cheek bones. Kelsey had dark brown hair, big brown doe eyes and braces for her soft overbite. She also said everything fast, as if in a hurry. It was just her speech pattern. Kelsey didn't care about any east/west rivalry, but did think the west was too loud while playing baseball in North Field. It bugged her most when she was trying to write her short stories or poems on the bleachers on south field, but she wasn't about to hold a grudge over that.

The only person she didn't like was Maggie Lyle, who lived in West Estates. However, that's not why Kelsey didn't like her. She didn't like her because Maggie was loud, obnoxious and would make fun of Kelsey's clothes, shoes and overbite. Maggie would call her "Princess" or "Ugly In Pink". Kelsey would always attack back in her notorious rapid fire speech by calling her "Tank Girl" or "Sasquatch".

Joy and Kelsey spent the next day of summer vacation at Cortney's house on Oval Court. They hung out, listened to music and bounced on Cortney's trampoline in the back yard. Joy announced that she had a soccer game on south field at two o'clock and had to go. She had her shin guards, socks and cleats with her in her backpack so she didn't have to go home first.

They said their goodbyes and the sisters walked up Oval Court then east on West Estates Way to Semicircle Drive. Of course, that took them right passed the Lyle House. Right on cue, Maggie Lyle came out of the garage and glared at Joy and Kelsey from the driveway.

Mary Margaret "Maggie" Lyle was not one to be messed with. A very stout girl with long blonde hair, round, plain face and hazel eyes, Maggie would say what she felt in a second without thinking about the consequences. She was even feared by most boys that knew her because her punch was as strong as any one of them. Since her dad was a veteran of the Iraqi war, she was also obsessed with all things military and was rarely seen without some sort of camouflage or military type clothing.

She was a fierce baseball player and competitor and very protective of her younger brother Timothy, whom everyone called "Little Timmy".

"Don't say a word, Kelsey, don't even look at her," Joy commanded.

They had just passed Maggie's house, when Maggie blurted out, "Hey Princess, nice purple sparkly shoes. Did you get them at the Thrift Store? I bet you paid, oh, let me guess, thirty cents for them?"

Kelsey, very quick with a rapid fire response, said, "Hey, see if you can guess who I am" as she simulated someone trying to catch a baseball and missing, smacking her forehead with her hand. This was in reference to a crucial fly ball Maggie missed at the fifth grade girls fast-pitch softball tournament at the local high school. The team could have gone to the state championships had Maggie not missed that fly ball. It was an incident well known throughout Buckeye Estates.

She provided a running commentary as she acted it out; "Oh, oh I got it, I got it, oh no I don't, I blew the whole thing" she yelled as her word spilled out as fast as a machine gun.

Maggie fumed, glaring daggers at Kelsey.

"C'mon, Kelsey," Joy said with authority and the two walked on. Maggie continued to glare at them as she went back in to the garage.

"Remember, we are in "enemy" territory," Joy said as she air quoted the word enemy.

"Whatever," Kelsey retorted.

About five houses down from the Lyles and across the street, Samantha Peckenpaugh came out of her garage just after Joy and Kelsey passed.

"Hey Sara, isn't that Julie and Leslie." Samantha said to her sister referring to two girls who lived over on Link Lane. Joy and Kelsey did resemble them from the back.

"I think so," replied Sara who stopped bouncing a basketball in the garage to come look at the two girls, who were already three houses down on West Estates Way.

"Let's get em!" Samantha said with a devious grin while holding some up unfilled water balloons.

"Yeah!!" Sara said with a sneer.

The Peckenpaugh kids consisted of Steven, Samantha, Sara and Shaun. All were skinny, athletic kids with brown hair and brown eyes but other than that, looked different in their own ways. They had a bit of a "red" streak running through them and could not stand any others from the east side of Buckeye Estates, no matter who they were. They were an ornery, tight-knit family that would stick together; if you messed with one Peckenpaugh, you messed with them all.

After they quickly filled up a handful of water balloons, Samantha and Sara crept down the other side of the street, ready to strike. When they came within a few car lengths behind the girls, Samantha gave the signal and they chucked the water balloons at Joy and Kelsey. Since both of the Peckenpaugh girls were excellent ball players with amazing arms and excellent aim, the balloons were right on target.

One hit Joy squarely on the back of her head and the other hit Kelsey on her back. It was enough to soak them both. They instinctively turned around to confront their attackers, their faces contorted out of confusion and dismay, as Samantha and Sara threw again, this time hitting Kelsey in the chest and Joy in the arm. In a split second, Samantha and Sara realized that they had a case of mistaken identity.

"Who are they?" Samantha whispered as she and Sara ducked behind a car, looking through the windows at the two bewildered girls.

"I dunno," Sara shrugged.

"I think they are "Others", said Samantha, "I've seen them at school, but they're definitely not Julie and Leslie."

"Uh oh!" they giggled in unison.

And as the Peckenpaugh girls crept back to their house in the west, Joy and Kelsey ran as fast as they could down the sidewalk to the path, trying not to get pelted again. They ran through North Field, across the bridge over the Divide, and to the safety of South Field where the Others were getting ready to play a pickup game of soccer.

The Peckenpaugh Girls realized their mistake but didn't think much more about it. They fully expected to jump out from behind the car and yell, "Gotcha!" at the girls as a harmless prank. What they didn't realize was that their mistake was going to help start a war.

CHAPTER 8
SOCCER ON SOUTH FIELD

The gang was all there in the south field. It was to be the first pick up soccer game of the summer vacation. All of the usual players from the east were there to play or hang out.

The Hammond Boys were there; Gregory and his two younger brothers. Their parents were from South Africa and were taught from a very early age that soccer was in their blood, and it showed. The Hammond boys were some of the best out there. They were fierce competitors and great all around athletes. Like the Peckenpaughs of the west, if you messed with one Hammond, you messed with them all.

Darin "Sneak" Coleman was also there. He was a slightly chunky kid with black hair and light freckles that could move a lot quicker that his build would suggest. Darin was nicknamed "Sneak" by his friends because of his ability to steal the soccer ball at will. He could seemingly be in one place on the field and, in the next second be clear across the field.

He was the best center they had. The same also applied off the field. You could be walking down the street with no one around or down the hall at school and Sneak would suddenly be beside you saying hi. Sneak could seemingly appear and disappear at will.

Everyone started to warm up and wait for the referees, Lexi and Maci. Lexi Riggs, Blake's sister and her best friend, Maci Childress were the ones who usually refereed the games. They were both in the 8th grade and since they both attended several soccer camps, and have played since second grade, they were usually asked to ref. They didn't mind because they both thought they had a better handle on the rules of the game and for the most part, didn't get much static from the others about the calls they made, except from Joy and Sneak.

Lexi and Maci were also the princesses of the east. Both were very pretty, wore the latest fashions and were very popular, especially with the boys of the east. Lexi had a very slender build with long slightly curly brown hair that some girls would kill for, a perfect complexion and light brown eyes. Maci was built the same way with bright blue eyes, naturally blond hair and cute dimples.

Several times play would stop as the girls walked up to get ready to officiate the game because they were mobbed by the boys. This day was no different. As Lexi and Maci walked they were surrounded by boys eager for them to even acknowledge their presence. The girls didn't mind and in fact, loved the attention.

As Lexi and Maci had the attention of almost every boy on the field, Blake didn't even have to turn around to know what was going on.

"Guys, quit freaking out about my sister" he whined. However, as he turned around his mood instantly changed, a smile came across his face as he said to himself "and her buddy Maci". Blake had a serious crush on Maci.

The girls on the field stood there glaring at the gathering of boys falling all over themselves and stammering over the two girls. They were irked that they had to wait to play, disgusted at the way the boys acted, and secretly jealous.

"This happens every time......every time," one of them blurted out.

I'm so sick of this," another girl chimed in. And with that, she raised her arm motioning for her teammate to administer the ball of justice. Taking the girl's lead, she took two steps back and kicked her soccer ball with all her might. The ball hit its mark on Jared's back.

Alright, we're gonna start to pick sides now," Jared said, turning around, mad as he tried to stretch the sting out of his back.

"What about Joy," Sneak asked, "I'm dying to show her up.......again."

"She will be here, she won't miss this," Blake answered.

Sneak was very cocky and he knew that Joy was his one real rival on the soccer field. The two were the best out there and although they talked smack to each other through every game, they secretly liked each other. They were also never on the same team because between the two of them, they could control entire games on South Field.

CHAPTER 9
"WE....GOT....HIT"

Joy and Kelsey tore into the South Field from one of the bridges across the Divide just as the east was about to choose sides. They no sooner got across the bridge when they stopped, out of breath, with their hands on their knees. Jared, sensing that they seemed upset, went over to them.

"What's going on, you guys look like you have seen a ghost," Jared chuckled as he said it.

"What did you do, fall in the divide," Greg teased, "You guys are all wet!"

"We....got....hit!" Joy blurted out between deep breaths.

"Hit?" Blake questioned.

"Yeah...... with water balloons...."

"You were attacked?" someone asked.

"I guess.... something, " Joy responded, her breath starting to return, but still trying to process what just happened.

"Hold on, sit over here and catch your breath," Lexi suggested to them. The two complied and sat down on the bleachers. "OK, now what happened? The girls were now surrounded by most of the kids on the field. Joy spoke first.

"We were just walking back from Rosie's on West Estates."

"Where at on West Estates?" Greg asked rather pointedly.

"We were almost to Semicircle drive by the…."

"And then??"

"We were pelted from behind with water balloons!"

"By whom?"

"We didn't see them," Joy continued, "We turned around and got hit again but no one was there."

"What do you mean 'No one was there?' Jared said, "somebody hit you."

"No," Joy argued, "whoever hit us was not around or they hid."

"I bet it was Maggie Lyle," Kelsey finally chimed in, in her own hyper speed delivery, "she somehow moved her fat body quickly across the street and followed us until she was close enough to hit us with water balloons because she has......"

"Kelsey, shut up!" Joy snapped, "she didn't follow us, I looked back and she went back in her house."

"Whatever," Kelsey hissed.

"So you saw Maggie Lyle?" Darin said.

"Ya," both girls said in unison,

"Did she say anything?" Maci asked.

"She started in on Kelsey shoes, like normal," Joy said.

"And I suppose you didn't say anything back, did you?" Greg said with a smirk, knowing very well Kelsey was not going to be quiet and give Maggie the upper hand. Kelsey looked annoyed at the question.

"Maggie couldn't have thrown all of those balloons at the same time anyways," Lexi said, "she would need some help."

"Plus she was way down the street. It wasn't her. I saw her walk back in to her house," Joy repeated persistently.

Jared wasn't saying anything at this point. He was silent, looking across the divide toward north field and the west beyond.

Everyone quit talking as Jared exclaimed to no one in particular, "so they want to play with water, huh?" as he kept gazing toward North field.

Blake, almost reading his mind, said, "So, what are we going to do about it?"

"We're gonna play our game," Jared said, "and then I want everyone back here at 7 O'clock, after dinner."

"Why?" some of the group chimed in.

"Something's got to be done and I have to get some maps," is all Jared would say.

CHAPTER 10
BASEBALL ON NORTH FIELD

"Anybody seen my ball glove?" Bode asked the group in the north field, "I can't find it at home."

"I ain't seen it, "Big Jessie said, "It had your name on it, right?"

"Yeah, did I leave it at your house?"

"Nah," Big Jessie answered.

It was the third day of summer vacation and the entire gang from the west was on hand for their normal pickup game of baseball. Maggie and Timmy Lyle were there first. They lived to play baseball. The Peckenpaughs came shortly after them, all four of them. All being awesome batters, they usually went to opposite sides as the teams were picked. All four were skinny, wiry athletes who didn't tire easily. Samantha was always picked to pitch because of her fastball and her unswerving accuracy.

Big Jessie was already in his catcher's gear. Mark Powell was on hand and ready to play, a fine all-around ball player. Combined with the rest of the kids that showed up, they actually had nine players per team this time.

"I couldn't find it at home, " Bode continued.

"Did you leave it here?" Mark inquired.

"I don't forget my glove," Bode answered.

"Who is that girl that plays with Cree and Brook?" Mark asked.

"That's Missy Hanson, Jared sister, she's an 'other'," "Big" Jessie answered.

"Cause I saw her the other day going towards south field with a ball glove," Mark said.

"Oh, really," Bode said inquisitively, his face tensed up.

"Well, it looked like a glove to me," Mark said.

"That girl wouldn't steal it," Steven Peckenpaugh piped up, "Would she?"

Bode thought about it for a second, "She's an 'Other', of course, she would take it. She probably took it to Jared."

"They don't play ball, they play soccer," someone interjected.

"Are you sure it was a glove?" Big Jessie asked.

"It looked like one to me," Mark said adamantly.

"If I catch him with my glove, man.........." Bode's voice trailed off, his fists clinched.

"Well, let's pick sides and play, we will sort this all out later," Big Jessie said, looking toward south field. "In the meantime, just use my spare." Big Jessie threw Bode his extra glove, sides were picked and the ball game was on.

CHAPTER 11
TO PREPARE FOR WAR

All of the others met at the edge of the soccer fields at 7PM as instructed. Jared walked up with a wave blaster and a bunch of papers. He started to draw a map in the dirt using the papers he brought with him as a guide. He was drawing a map of Buckeye Estates West in the dirt. As everyone gathered around, Jared didn't say a word. When he was finished, he explained,

"This is West Estates; this is how we plan our attack."

"Attack, what do you mean attack?" Blake piped up; confusion was written all over his face.

"They attacked us, we attack them."

"Cool, I'm in!" Lexi piped up.

"Yep, we're there," chimed in the Hammond boys.

"So am I," said Blake.

"Count us in," came responses from some others in attendance.

"We're in," a couple of other kids said in unison.

Most everyone on South Field that evening was in agreement, the west needed to be attacked. Of course, Joy wasn't convinced.

"What, we're gonna invade West Estates?" Joy said sarcastically, rolling her eyes.

"Can we just attack Maggie Lyle and call it a day!" Kelsey said with a smile, Joy glared at her.

"I ain't going over there," Darin said with a look of fear on this face.

"Oh, so you liked looking stupid, dripping wet, standing on West Estates?" Jared said to Joy very pointedly.

"I've never seen either of you run like that, you were scared," Blake interjected.

"You were both white as a clean sheet when you came running back here," Greg pointed out.

"This is stupid," Joy fired back, "it was just a joke; don't you think if it was serious they would have used something other than water balloons!"

"Then why did you run?" someone asked.

"Because we were startled and didn't want to get hit again," Joy explained even more persistently than before. "I didn't really want to be soaking wet and try to play a soccer game, Duh." She emphasized 'Duh' as she said it.

"Did the balloons hurt?" Jared asked.

"Kinda," Joy said.

"They did," Kelsey chimed in.

"Ha, some joke," Maci said, her arms crossed, looking perturbed as she stared at Joy.

"Well, I'm not gonna start some war just because of a ...."

"You didn't start anything," Blake cut Joy off in mid-sentence, getting louder as he said it.

"We're not gonna stand around and let our side be attacked for walking down the street, that's punked," Greg spoke up.

"What sides?" Joy began to yell, "you guys act like this is some revenge thing or some dramatic war, it was just water balloons."

"Maybe it is revenge," Maci said, "if I got hit with a water balloon for no reason I would......"

"Take it as a prank," Joy questioned.

"They hit you, they hit me too," Lexi fired back.

"Dudes, I ain't going over there," Sneak repeated loudly.

"Well you can leave us out of your little holy war," Joy's face was beet red as she got up to leave, "Stupid," was all she could get out.

"I'm in if it means Maggie Lyle gets pelted with………," Kelsey started to say.

"Kelsey, c'mon," Joy commanded, cutting her off.

"I gotta go," Kelsey muttered as she got up and meekly followed her big sister home.

A few kids briefly tried to stop them.

"Let'em go," Jared said, "they would just be in the way, besides, we need to go over the plan of attack."

"Um, aren't we doing this for them?" someone exclaimed.

"No, we're not," Jared said, "we're doing this for the East."

"So what are we going to attack with?" Blake asked.

"They want to fight with water, we'll fight with water," Jared said holding up his wave blaster, a determined look across with face.

"We all have these," Jared continued, "or can get one, right?"

The crowd nodded and a few "yeah's" could be heard.

"Mine shoots pretty far, full auto and I bet yours do too, right?" Jared was getting louder. There were more "yeah's" from the kids and a little bit louder.

"And I don't think any one of us is gonna sit here and let anyone from our side just get attacked and not do anything about it, right?" Jared was now yelling, his face more animated with anger. Jared knew his audience.

"Yeah!!" responded the kids from the east, matching his volume.

"I'm not just gonna sit here and I bet I know who attacked Joy and Kesley and you do too," Jared had the kids in a frenzy as they all started to yell and scream in support.

"Sooo.....," Blake said with some hesitation, "who do you think did this?"

"It had to be Bode," Jared said, his eyes staring straight into Blake's, "The guy will do anything to make us look bad, him and Big Jessie."

"He wouldn't attack girls that don't.............."

"Yes, he would, he would probably pelt your baby sister Carrie with a water balloon if he had the chance," Sneak was cut off by Jared's searing words. Sneak just shook his head, but listened to their leader.

"So here is my plan," Jared said much more calmly now, directing the crowd to look at the drawing of west estates in the dirt. Jared had the plan all figured out. He had squads drawn up, key kids to attack and where they lived, how to attack and an escape plan.

"So, we just gonna use wave blasters?" someone inquired.

"Nope, we got these too," Jared produced a plastic bag from the Sterling Shop and Save filled with water balloons."

"If you hold it by one side you can grab the balloons like this," and Jared demonstrated by holding one side of the handle of the plastic bag while thrusting his hand into the open part of the bag, grabbing a water balloon, and hurling it at the back wall of the strip mall. He continued his demonstration, hurling balloon after balloon with speed and precision, determined look on his face. The group was impressed. Jared further explained that the water balloons would be for the initial sneak attack, the wave blasters were for the follow up, the final blow.

"Now for our plan of attack," Jared directed the group to the map he had drawn in the dirt. At this point some of the group bowed out and went home, but the core group remained.

Jared had planes for three squads, A, B and C, as he explained the attack plan. He sounded like he was describing a play for a soccer or football game; it was the only way he knew how.

Squad "A" consisted of Jared and three other kids. They would attack through the far path, up Semicircle to West Estates Way, hitting Big Jessie Taylor and up to Stem Road, where Bode Catron lived.

They would be deep into enemy territory, he explained, as though quoting some war movie. They would then backtrack to West Estates Way and hit Mark Powell as they headed to the bridge over the Divide, back to East Estate and safety.

Squad "B" consisted of four other kids and Sneak. They had a tough mission; hit the Peckenpaughs on West Estates Way.

The Peckenpaughs would be most likely be heavily armed and would probably return fire. It they could, pelt any other kid they saw on the way back to the closest path off of Semicircle that leads to North Field. Sneak sat there still shaking his head as Jared continued to explain.

Squad "C" would consist of all three Hammond boys. Their strategy was simple; cross the Divide on East Estates Way, soldier on through to Creekside Court to take care of any of the kids that lived there and then backtrack to East Estates. The Hammond boys volunteered for this assignment. The rest would stay behind near the Divide and act as backup in case any squad was chased.

When Jared was done explaining the plan of attack, it took about five seconds for everyone to start talking at once.

"Wait, wait, wait!" Greg spoke up, "How are we going know if they are going be home?"

"How do we know they're gonna be outside?" Blake questioned, "Or even out front."

"I aint' ringin' no doorbells only to pelt someone in the face with a water balloon," Greg said adamantly.

"Where do me and Maci fit into this plan?" Lexi complained.

"I still AIN"T going over there!" Sneak shouted.

"Don't you think they would warn each other if they saw us coming?" Blake said.

At this point the group started to openly make fun of the elaborate plan Jared had come up with.

"Ya, we just wander around West Estates in a big group with wave blasters, no one will notice that," Blake said sarcastically.

"It's a lame plan!" Maci said flatly.

"I'll knock on the door and be like, excuse me but could you step out of the way while I soak your son with this wave blaster," Greg said between laughs.

"Hope you don't mind the water on the walls and floor," someone else howled.

"Alright, alright, alright," Jared yelled, clearly agitated. "Do any of you brain children have a better suggestion," he said with a smirk.

"Easy, why don't we just wait till they play baseball again," Maci said shrugging her shoulders and holding out her hands.

Everyone thought for a moment. Blake was the first to speak, "We don't know when they play, there's no set time."

"We might be waiting a while," Greg said.

Jared pondered on this for a minute and finally spoke up. "Ya know, Maci is right, they will all be in the same place at the same time," he continued, "We know they play in the mornings sometimes, but they always play in the afternoon, after lunch, and I just thought of a plan to see where everyone is at." He looked right at Sneak.

"What are we gonna do, wait here and then attack as their playing?" someone asked.

"No, they will be too spread out, we wait until they start to choose sides and then we attack," a weird smile came over Jared's face. "We would have to be ready and go over right after they start," Jared's mind was now moving a million miles a minute.

"I'm not thrilled about standing around on Semicircle with a wave wlaster in my hands, waiting to be picked off," someone retorted.

"We wouldn't, we would wait here for Sneak's text."

"What???" Sneak jumped to his feet.

"Sneak, you could go over there and come back and tell us where everyone is before we attack."

"You didn't hear me," Sneak shouted, "I'm not going over there!!!"
It was time for Blake to make a sacrifice.

"Would you do it for my new copy of "Boundary Infringement 3; walkthrough and game guide"?" Blake asked.

Everyone who knew video games gasped. They knew they game had just come out a week ago. The game guide alone was hard to get. Blake also knew Sneak's weakness; video games, especially Boundary Infringement.

Sneak suddenly calmed down, "The complete walkthrough guide?"

"Yep," Blake smiled.

"How…." he stammered, "did you get it, the game just came out. I don't even have it yet!"

"I just won it in a raffle at Gamer's Haven in the mall," Blake shot a sly look at Sneak.

"Would that be worth it?" Blake said, confident look on his face.

"Ummmm," Sneak said matter of factly, "I could probably do it for that."

CHAPTER 12
IMPERSONATING DORKBOY

With the bribe, Sneak was on board. He was to go over right after lunch and see when the west started heading toward North Field. He would text Jared who would assemble the squads.

"How are you going to blend in over there?" Blake asked.

"Easy, I'll dress up like Dorkboy."

David Boerner was the youngest kid in the Boerner family and lived on the Boerner farm which is right next to Boerner's Field. David was a strange one, at least to the kids of Buckeye Estates. He was good-looking kid, slender with sandy blonde hair that kinda hung over his brown eyes. He always wore the same glasses, flannel shirt, ball cap advertising some type of seed or fertilizer and cowboy boots. He only had a few friends and kept to himself at school, but it was how he acted at home that earned him the nickname, "Dorkboy."

He would lay on the edge of the field among the soybeans. Other times he would run back and forth, screaming only to fall down suddenly. Other times he would bend over and start smacking his own butt with both hands.

Still other times he would do weird karate type moves that were foreign to the kids of Buckeye Estates so they didn't really know what he was doing.

When the ball diamond was empty, he would go out and play baseball by himself, throwing the ball up and catching it or hitting it. It got boring quickly, but he was too shy to ask to play and no one thought to ask him. Since he was painfully shy, his weird actions were his way of gaining attention.

Sneak dressed up in his disguise right after lunch. Sure close up, he could not pass as Dorkboy, but Sneak wouldn't let anybody get that close to him. Plus, they knew Dorkboy had a friend that lived in West Estates so no one would probably pay attention anyways. Sneak's mission was simple; walk around the west and text Jared when kids started heading towards North Field. The east would have to strike quickly soon after the West kids got there. They wanted them on the side all together and not spread out in the field.

Sneak started out walking along the field. He played the role well, running as fast as he could only to fall down. Even though there were just a few kids in the North field, they paid no attention. Cree, Brook and Missy were on the playground, but they didn't care, they were too busy singing. Sneak would go into his karate chop moves, walk really fast then turn and go the other way for a bit and fall down.

David watched this charade for a bit, laughing at the kid on the edge of his family's field.

"Nah, he's got it all wrong, I would have fallen down more," David thought and laughed as he watched. They didn't know he was actually practicing his martial arts exercises; smacking his own butt was for attention.

Sneak made it through the field, down the far path and onto Semicircle Drive. It took him a while to act out the Dorkboy bit but he was now on Semicircle. That meant he was now behind enemy lines. He was scared, but knew he had a job to do. He went up Semicircle past Long Court to West Estates, then down West Estates to Stem Road. No kids in sight. Up Stem Road, he walked to the intersection of West and East "Y" Roads and back down the other side of Stem Road.

"Ghost town" Sneak thought. Some kids came out of a house on Stem Road. Sneak didn't recognize them, but turned, crossed the street and went up Stem Road, the opposite direction of North Field. "No dice," he thought. He went back down Stem Road to West Estate and started west. He was just about to give up when the Peckenpaughs poured out of their house, got on their bikes, ball gloves and bats in hand and headed down West Estate to Semicircle. They were going to North Field.

"Finally," Sneak thought, "something to report." He crossed West Estate and the Peckenpaughs rode by, paying him no mind.

Just then, Bode Catron and Big Jessie started walking down Link Lane towards Semicircle. Then Maggie Lyle came out. "Okay, this is getting good", Sneak thought, "it's obvious they're going to play some ball".

"What is taking him so long?" Greg finally spoke up.

All of the others were congregated on the south path, just out of view from North field. They were all geared up, ready for Sneak's text. They had seven wave blasters among them and ten sacks of water balloons. They were ready to launch the attack.

"He will text us, we have to give him more time," Jared answered. No sooner than he said that, the call, not a text, came in.

"Where are you?" Jared answered his call.

"Stem Road and West Estates, the Peckenpaughs, Bode, Jessie and Maggie Lyle are headed toward North Field and here comes some more now, all with ball gloves and bats," Sneak reported as he crossed the street away from them.

Jared ended the phone call, "Its time."

Everyone scrambled to their feet, wave blasters and water balloons in hand. They headed north up Delightful Lane, Jared spouting instruction the whole way.

"Our attack has gotta be swift, we gotta be in and out before they know it. Choose your targets quickly. I don't care who you hit, just leave Bode to me.

The group paused at the path off of Semicircle Drive leading to North Field. "Lexi, Maci, you know what you have to do, right?" Jared asked.

"Yep," Lexi replied, "Stay behind and pelt the stragglers." She said that with a proud smile.

CHAPTER 13
THE "OTHERS" ATTACK

Most of the west kids at that time were already on North field, talking and warming up. Bode and Big Jessie stood side by side ready to choose sides. They flipped a quarter and Bode won the toss. Bode spoke up, "I'll take….."

The East stuck quickly, Blake threw first, striking Big Jessie right in the chest followed by a steady stream of water from his wave blaster. Some others moved toward the far side of the back stop, throwing a continuous barrage of water balloons, one kid's head reeled back with the force of the blow, being hit twice square in the face. Greg and his brothers made a dead set for the Peckenpaughs, hitting Steven and Samuel before they even knew what was happening. Bode now turned toward the onslaught unfolding before him. Jared, true to his word, threw a balloon that hit Bode right in the face. Someone barely got out, "Others," before his mouth was filled with water and bits of rubber.

Big Jessie reeled back on to clear his eyes from the water before he was hit again. Maggie turned toward the path only to be smacked in the arm followed by water to the face and chest. She was dazed for a second.

Bode started toward the path, still not seeing too clearly as water was still in his eyes. As he rubbed the water out, he could see Jared in front of him. Their eyes met briefly as Jared, a determined sneer on his face, threw another balloon as hard as he could. The balloon hit Bode's leg followed by a wave blaster assault. Bode had no time to clear his eyes. He, like the rest of the kids couldn't see very clearly because of the onslaught of water to the face from the wave blasters and the balloons that hit their mark. Meanwhile, the Hammond Boys pelted Samantha, Sara and Shawn mercilessly. They could barely recover from a hit when they were hit again. The balloons kept coming followed by hard streams of water from the wave blasters. One girl was actually knocked off balance by the force of the balloons that someone threw. She fell into the dirt which was quickly turning to mud.

Some of the balloons were not breaking on impact and Steven was the first to actually pick one up and counter attack. He started toward is attackers as he threw the balloon. He wanted to hit, but not with water balloons, but with his fists. His first offensive was cut short. Two rounds of water balloons met his advance followed by several hits from three different wave blasters. He could barely see. More kids were now picking up unbroken water balloons and returning fire but the damage was already done.

Meanwhile, Lexi and Maci guarded their post by the path on Semicircle. Pelt the stragglers were their orders and that is exactly what they were going to do until they got the call to return to East Estates.

Mark Powell and two of his friends from another neighborhood came wandering down Semicircle Drive. Lexi and Maci were right on cue; they hid behind a car until they were within striking distance. They blasted all three without mercy, Lexi with balloons, Maci with a wave blaster.

All that Mark and his two friends could do was yell that they were gonna be sorry. Dripping wet, they started to chase the two girls but Lexi and Maci were too fast and were halfway down Semicircle Drive before the boys could react.

That's when they spotted Timmy Lyle. He had just turned on to the street, riding his bike to North Field. The two girls had behind a car in the street until he got close enough.

Little Timmy, Maggie's little brother was a blonde haired kid with glasses who was pretty quiet. He didn't start any trouble. In fact, you never heard a peep out of him. All that he wanted to do was play baseball, ride his bike and climb anything that could get him past five feet in the air. He would climb things most people would shy away from and had excellent balance. However, just like his older sister Maggie, Little Timmy did not like any of the older kids from the east.

When he was within ten feet, Lexi burst out from in front of the car, "HEY YOU!" she yelled and threw the water balloon with all her might. Timmy looked up and the water balloon hit him full in the face. The force threw his head back, his glasses went flying and the handlebars of the bike twisted, sending Timmy reeling off the bike. His head hit the grass median between the street and the sidewalk with a thud, and bounced.

Lexi winced when she saw what she had done as well as Maci. By unspoken agreement, the two turned quickly and sprinted down Semicircle Drive to West Estates Way, then east across the Divide to the safety of East Estates Way. Once in the east, they jogged down Delightful Lane to the rendezvous point.

The main strike force had the west in complete disarray. The Peckenpaughs could barely see from the water, Steven blindly staggered toward the attackers only to be blinded again. Jared and a few others pelted Bode several more times. Maggie could barely breath because of all the water and bits of water balloon in her mouth.

Jared gave the signal and just like that, it was over. In vain Bode tried to chase them but it was. When he cleared his eyes, all he could see was butts and elbows heading south toward South Field. They ran past the playground where the Playground Three were playing, cheering, laughing and pointing at the battle that just unfolded. They ran to the path by the lone oak tree, across the Divide to South Field, and safety.

Because the east had hit so hard and so fast, the west kids were completely dumbfounded. A few more tried to run after the attackers, but they were long gone.

Bode came walking back from his failed chase, eyes blazing. Off in the distance they could hear the others celebrating, whooping and cheering. Bode looked at everyone square in the eyes. Everyone was soaking wet. No one escaped a least one hit, no one had time to react, and no one had time to retaliate except for chucking a few unbroken balloons back at them, all to no avail. It was over before it had begun.

Meanwhile, Timmy pulled himself off the ground, still in a bit of a daze. It took him a minute to find his glasses because they had flown pretty far into the street, and one lens had popped out.

CHAPTER 14
AFTERMATH

Everyone was talking at once, some were wondering why they attacked for no reason, some were talking about how fast the attack was and some were already talking revenge. Bode looked right at his main man, "Big" Jessie. They were both thinking the same thing. They didn't even need to speak.

Mark and his buddies came walking up, clothes drenched from their attack. He explained that they were ambushed on Semicircle by two girls. As he looked around, he didn't need to ask what happened to the rest. Their dazed look, dripping wet hair and splotches of wet dirt told the whole story.

Just then little Timmy came walking up, dripping wet, wheeling his bike with him. The welt on his cheek was getting darker and darker by the second. Big sister, Maggie as well as a few others went over to him.

"What happened?" Maggie gasped.

"Some girl hit me with a water balloon in the face real hard!" Timmy sobbed.

"What girl?" Maggie asked, her face turned into an angry cringe.

"I didn't really see her, my glasses got knocked off my face," he answered, "but there were two of 'em."

"Didn't you say two girls pelted you?" Big Jessie asked Mark.

"Where were you at, Timmy?" Steven Peckenpaugh asked.

"On Semicircle."

"Yep, and it's probably a safe bet it was the same two girls," Mark answered.

"What did they look like," someone asked but Mark and his friends all agreed that they didn't get a very good look at them.

Maggie, fuming at this point, had heard enough. She started to walk across North Field but was stopped by Big Jessie.

"C'mon Maggie, we don't even know who she is," he reasoned.

"I don't care, I'll beat up every one of them who happens to be a girl that should narrow it down huh?" She continued to walk towards South Field. She continued "wait till I get my hands on Kelsey, she probably did it!" her fists were clinched.

"Maggie, "Big Jessie reasoned, "Kelsey Shaw couldn't throw anything over ten feet, let alone a water balloon, it wasn't her."

Big Jessie urged her back, "Maggie, we need a plan, besides you ain't gonna take on the entire East."

"I will if I have to," she responded.

"C'mon girl, we need you back here," Big Jessie said.

Maggie and Big Jessie really liked each other and he was the only one who could talk sense into her. She complied, walking back to the group, looking over her shoulder as the shouts and cheers from the "Others" slowly subside.

The whole group was now looking at Bode for an answer.

"Now what?" someone asked.

"We meet at the Pit tonight at 7:00," Bode told them. And with that, he started to walk towards the far path.

"So are we gonna play some ball or what, it's just water!" one of Mark's buddies spoke up. Since he wasn't from Buckeye Estates, he didn't understand the severity of what just happened.

Bode stopped for a second, without turning around, he answered, "You go ahead, I don't feel much like play ball right now," and continued on toward the far path.

CHAPTER 15
VICTORY CELEBRATION

The others regrouped on the south path leading to Delightful Lane. They were whooping, hollering and celebrating their rapid- fire attack. Everything went exactly as planned. The attack force moved like a well-oiled machine, proud of their victory.

"Man, we caught them with their pants down!" Greg said, smiling from ear to ear.

"Did you see the look on their faces?" someone beamed, "we smacked them good!"

"We all did exactly what we were supposed to, good job guys," Jared said, one eye looking toward North Field.

"They got to realize not to mess with 'the Others'!" Blake put an emphasis on his voice when he said it. He started to chant "Others"

"Others......Others......Others!" they began to chant in unison.

"We ain't nothing to be messed with," Thomas Hammond shouted.

"We tore 'em up," someone shouted.

"You know they are going to counterattack," Blake looked right at Jared with a grin on his face.

"Let'em," Jared replied with a scowl on his face. "We will be ready and besides the look on Bode's face will be worth it if they do!"

Lexi and Maci came walking up, out of breath because they ran most of the way there. They didn't look happy.

"What's the matter? Did you run into trouble?" Greg asked.

"No.........well, sorta."

"Who did ya smack?" one boy asked with a huge smile on his face.

"We got Mark Powell and two guys, I don't know their names but I think they live in Killdeer Acres," Maci said.

"I also hit Timmy Lyle pretty hard," Lexi admitted, not looking too proud about it.

"What's wrong with that?" Greg asked with a shrug and a smile.

"Well..........I knocked his glasses off and he fell off his bike and hit his head."

"Was he still moving?" Greg asked.

"Yeah," Lexi replied.

"Then he's okay," Greg blurted out, half laughing through his answer.

"Hey, you didn't hit him, he got in the way of your throw!" someone bellowed.

This was followed by more shouts and cheers from the group. They were jumping up and down and high-fiving each other. Lexi and Maci didn't join in the celebration. They were still reeling from what just happened. Neither did Jared at this point. He was looking toward North field, watching the tiny figures off in the distance slowly walk towards their homes.

"Let'em counterattack!" he said to himself, gritting his teeth.

CHAPTER 16
"WHOEVER FIGHTS MONSTERS"

After dinner, Bode spent the next hour or so in his room alone, fuming, thinking and planning. His thoughts were interrupted by Brooks's voice downstairs, enthusiastically telling their mom about the water balloon fight.

"Oh you should have seen it, Mom, balloons were flying, kids were running and SPLAT! SPLAT! SPLAT! We wanted to join in but it was over so fast".

As she reenacted the fight in the kitchen for her mom, her arms were flailing as she described the fight, running back and forth, so her mom would get the full effect. She didn't realize it was a one-sided fight and it wasn't for fun.

"Brook, SHUT UP!" Bode yelled down the stairs.

"Hey Bode, come down here, I want to talk to you," Mrs. Catron yelled from the kitchen.

Bode pointed at Brook with a "shut up" look on this face as he passed her going toward the kitchen. Brooklyn stuck out her tongue in response on her way to the back yard. He jabbed at her and she ran out the back door.

Faith Catron had a very commanding presence to her. She had a soft Kentucky accent and didn't get riled up, but when she talked, she spoke with conviction. When she made a point, people listened to her, especially her kids. Today, however, was an exception.

"Brooklyn tells me you had a little water balloon fight today," Mrs. Catron said.

"It wasn't' a little fight, we got attacked," Bode replied sarcastically, looking at his mom, an expression of anger and frustration on his face.

"So tell me what happened," Mrs. Catron said.

Bode described how they were starting to pick sides for baseball and the "Others" came out of nowhere and started chucking water balloons at them, as well as shooting them with wave blasters.

"Ya know, Bode, it sounds like a harmless prank, no one was hurt, it was……."

"No one was hurt?" Bode cut his mom off, "what about Little Timmy, that's not hurt?"

"What happened to Timmy?"

"Some girl hit him so hard it put a welt on his face, knocked him off of his bike and broke his glasses! What about that?" Bode started to get loud.

"Calm it down," Mrs. Catron said with anger and authority in her voice.

"It was probably a brick inside of a balloon" he muttered.

"Nonsense Bode, I know how you feel about the kids from East Estates, especially Jared." She sounded perturbed as if her son didn't give her enough credit to know this.

"Yeah, 'Others,'" Bode said disgustedly.

"Others, try human beings".

"I guess so, about the human part I mean" at this point Bode refused to look his mom in the eye.

"Listen to me now, Bode" she said sternly. "You're picking a fight with kids who are not your enemy." Her finger was right in his face. He still refused to look his mom in the eye. "This little rift you have with them is only going to get worse".

Mrs. Catron calmed down a bit, her voice returning to normal. Because she was a philosophy professor at the Ohio State University, she would always incorporate famous quotes to enhance her life lessons.

"A writer of some ability once wrote" she began, "something to the effect of when you go in search of monsters, don't become one yourself."

Her words hung in the air of the kitchen, "don't let this consume you, Bode, it's going to end badly if you do." Mrs. Catron was done.

"Can I go now?" Bode asked defiantly, a bored look on his face.

"Yeah, you can go, where are you headed?"

"To the basketball courts" Bode lied. He had a meeting at the Pit.

"Hey!" Mrs. Catron called after him, "your birthday is coming up, any suggestions?" she said, trying to lighten the mood.

Bode paused in the front doorway, "A new ball glove would be nice......to replace the one they stole!" Bode walked out the front door and headed to the Pit.

CHAPTER 17
MEETING AT THE PIT

The west kids gathered in the pit that night. Of course, by now most of Boerner's field was pretty quiet, with just a few kids playing on the playground.

The "Pit" was an old borrow pit at the North edge of Boerner's Field and the Farm. It was created because they needed dirt for the bridges across 13 Pole Creek. It was really just a low spot that became a small pond in the spring, became a dry pit in the summer and sometimes an ice skating rink in the winter. The west kids could meet there and talk without being heard. Most were already gathered by the time Bode walked up.

"What do you think started that?" Big Jessie started.

"Well, something started it and why water balloons?" someone asked. Samantha elbowed Sara in the side, stern look on her face, making sure she didn't say a word.

"Man, I can't believe how fast they were!" Shaun said.

"And how hard they threw," Steven, his older brother added.

"Those wimps play soccer, not baseball" someone added.

"That was planned out, they didn't just attack out of the blue," Big Jessie said.

Maggie and Timmy Lyle just sat there looking straight ahead, Maggie looking angrier by the second, Timmy more dismayed. The frustration and anger grew with every second, the bruise on his check turning darker and darker.

"Because they're too wimpy for any other kinda fight," Mark piped up, addressing Big Jessies statements.

"So, they wanna play with water?" Bode finally spoke up.

"I'm not playin' anymore," Maggie finally belted out as she stood up.

"Hold on, Maggie," Bode commanded, "Steven, do you still have that water balloon launcher you made last summer? The one that can shoot really far?"

"Sure do, just shot it the other day!"

"Can you make some more?"

"I could; I would need some tubing and I think I have some springs lying around."

Steven was a master tinkerer. He was always dismantling stuff, building things and messing with devices in his garage. Since his dad was a mechanic and a welder, Steven usually had plenty of his stuff at his disposal to play with. He once pulled an old lawn mower apart and, with scrap metal tubing and the engine, he made a mini bike. If anyone out of the group could construct something, it was Steven.

"What kinda tubes?" Bode asked.

"I like plastic ones, like the kind for water pipes, but I could make ones out of the paper ones that posters come in. They won't last that long though."

"You wanna attack them?" Mark voice trailed off.

Bode held up his finger, indicating for Mark to hold on. He looked around at everyone when he did.

"How long would it take to make some?" Bode looked back at Steven.

"Depends on how many you want." Steven said. Bode looked around at the group and his expression on his face indicated that he was counting.

"What about ten?"

"Whoa, that's a lot, I might have enough stuff to make about four."

"How long?" Bode asked again.

"At least a week."

"How about three days?" Bode said in the form of a question, but it was really a command.

By now the kids started talking amongst themselves. A murmur started to rise. Some started to shoot questions at Bode.

"Hold on, I have a plan," Bode assured them. However, some like Maggie, Mark and Big Jessie wanted to attack right now, or at least tomorrow. Bode explained that it would be good it they waited. That would make the others think that they had decided not to attack, had forgotten or were too scared. Bode was cunning. He knew, or at least thought he knew that the east would not attack a second time. He also would use the football strategies that his Junior Football League couch would always use; Do exactly the opposite of the obvious next play.

"I'm gonna need some help," Steven said.

"Ok, so we got about a couple of days, we all need to think about where we can get the stuff that Steven needs. Look in your garages, can you all do that?" the group nodded. "We're not gonna just forget about today, right?" The group agreed.

"We need a plan and I have one," the group started to cheer as Bode became more excited.

"We are gonna hit faster and harder than they did, and catch'em totally off guard."

The entire group was now nodding and fired up. Bode began to draw in the dirt. He was drawing a map of Boerner's Field. The west gathered around as Bode explained his plan. His plan was simple. The shrubs and bushes along the divide were, by now, thick and tall enough to hide behind. If they were to sneak up from the edge of Boerner's Farm, they could not be seen from South field. They would have to crawl most of the way and set themselves up along the divide. Once set up, they could stand up on Bode's signal and fire at will.

He also wanted to tack boards on the side of the oak near the east bridge. He wanted people in the oak tree so if any "Others" tried to come across in retaliation, they could jump down and hold them off. They could drop from the lowest branches of the oak which was about five to six feet.

They would need someone agile. It was decided that Samantha would go up in the oak. The lowest branches of the oak had enough leaves to hide them. Once down, Bode and a few other kids could be near to help pelt anybody that came across that bridge. They would position Shawn and Timmy at the far bridge in case anyone went that way. Timmy balked at this, saying he wanted be part of the main group. Bode thought about it for a second and agreed. He thought it would also be appropriated if Timmy fired the first shot. They all realized that the timing of the attack depended on when Steven could get the water balloon launchers made. Steven knew his task and would get right to work.

"Oh, there's one more thing," Bode said as they all started to leave. He had been holding a water balloon in his hand the whole time. Now he raised it above his head and threw it on the ground. It exploded and the water inside was bright pink. Everyone stared at the pink splatter on the ground, little bits of blue rubber from the balloon lying in the spot.

"That's dye my Dad uses at his work," Bode exclaimed proudly. "They're gonna know we have been there cause were gonna paint them pink!" This got laughs and nods of approval from the group.

As they were breaking up, Rosie, walking her dog, came up on Bode, Big Jessie, Steven and Samantha still talking.

"Hey guys, what's up?" She inquired cheerfully.

"Nothing you need to know," Big Jessie sneered. Rosie was taken aback by the snide comment. Big Jessie was always so nice to her but on this night; he had an edge to him.

"What do you mean?" she asked a little hurt.

"Nothing, just go hang out with your little buddies," Samantha glared at her.

"What are you talking about?" Rosie was caught completely off guard.

"Oh, you know, Joy and Kelsey, the ones that walk through here spying on everyone," Samantha shot back. "Maggie said they always walk through here checking stuff out."

"Spying? Are you serious? I think all this war crap has warped your brains," she was getting mad.

"Look, those are my friends, they don't care about this stupid rivalry crap and neither do I. Plus, last I heard Estates Way is a public street that anyone can walk on. It was probably you dorks that pelted them with water balloons in the first place."

"Whaaaat?" Steven said with a scowl on his face. "What do you mean, who pelted them because it sure was not us?"

Samantha remained silent.

"Ya, like you don't know," Rosie said sarcastically.

"Ya right," Big Jessie retorted, "they made that up to get an excuse to attack us today. None of us would just smack people with balloons."

Samantha was as quiet as a mouse.

"Attack? what attack?" Rosie asked in confusion. She really didn't know about the earlier attack. Joy had told her that Jared was thinking about it, but didn't know it had happened.

"You know what I'm talking about." Big Jessie continued.

Bode remained silent this whole time, both eyes on Rosie. Steven and Big Jessie just shook their heads and scoffed. They started to walk away. Rosie's cheeks were beet red as she tried to defend her friends. She started to walk away too.

"Oh, and Rosie," Bode said angrily as she started to leave, "you need to figure out which side you are really on." His voice and face conveyed rage. She stopped and turned around to face him. The sheer meanness in his voice hurt her feelings.

The West would go to the pit so they wouldn't be heard. But that night they were heard. David Boerner lay just inside Boerner's Field where the weeds on the edge of the field concealed him.

David had heard every word that was said. He had seen them all gather in the Pit and snuck up to eavesdrop. As everyone left, he made his escape; he said to himself, "Man, I can't miss that!" As he snuck away, one thing did concern him.............Kelsey.

"I don't want to see her get hurt," he thought to himself. "I gotta find a way to warn her."

CHAPTER 18
STEVEN GOES TO WORK

Steven immediately began constructing the water balloon launchers. He had constructed his own from watching videos online. It could launch pretty far and could send two or three balloons flying at once. It could definitely launch them over the divide and onto the soccer fields.

In the next few days kids brought him all sorts of tubes. Some were plastic and some were thick poster tubes. With these he would place a spring inside the tube and attach it to a handle through a slit on the side. He also made pistol-like grips out of small pieces of two-by-fours. Then the handle was pulled back, a balloon was dropped in the tube and launched. The problem was this kept breaking the balloons before they left the tube. He made up for this by attaching a kind of shelf on the spring for the balloons to sit on until it left the end of the tube. It was also a pain to try and hold the handle back with one hand and load the balloons with the other. The solution was to install triggers.

This was easier than he thought. His dad had a shop set up in the garage with all sorts of metal parts for Steven to use. He had some metal clips that would hold the handle back until you unclipped it. He attached these to the outside of the tubes with sheet metal and screws. The cardboard tubes would not last as long as the plastic ones obviously, but they would make it through the battle.

Of course, balloon launchers were sold in stores but no one had any money and they would not work as well as anything Steven could make. They definitely would not launch as hard and as far. The kids had a theory, that since the store bought launchers were made by adults who were too busy thinking about safety, they just didn't have the hitting power that homemade ones had. The adults also tell kids not to point them at anyone but kids knew that was not only half the fun of it, but that was why they were made.

Meanwhile, Bode was busy finding all of the pink dye that he could.

CHAPTER 19
FINAL PREPERATION

A couple of days after the meeting at the pit, a couple of kids chucked water balloons from the divide at some ball players in north field. When the kids who got hit ran after them, the kids took off like gazelles being hunted and nobody really saw who they were. Word got around West Estates that three kids were also pelted with balloons as they walked across the bridge on Estate Way. Again, the perpetrators were hiding in the bushes that lined the Divide. Both times no one could figure out who did it and to this day, no one has ever 'fessed up. However, the message was clear. The "Others" could seemingly attack at will with no retaliation.

"That's OK," Bode said to the group after a ball game, "Let them think that we ain't gonna do nothing."

With the help of his sisters and brother as well as other kids from the west, Steven managed to finish ten launchers in record time. They also had another seven wave blasters at their disposal. West Estates was prepared for a counter offensive.

A meeting was held at the pit that night. Someone had looked at the forecast on the internet and found out that it was not supposed to rain at all that week. A test was made of all launchers and wave blasters and every weapon checked out. Three of the launchers didn't have a trigger mechanism so someone else would have to put the balloons down the tube while another person fired them. Steven just could not find the parts to make triggers and ran out of clips. It was decided that as few of the younger kids would load the balloons while someone else shot it.

Bode had all of the dye at the ready. Somebody piped up with the idea of using paint guns but that was quickly shot down due to cost of gas, paintballs and the fact that not many of the kids had paint guns. Someone else interjected that paint balls can really hurt someone without the protective gear and helmet on. This statement was met with a bunch of so-what looks.

At the end of the meeting it was decided that tomorrow would be the day to attack. They didn't want to wait any longer or have a bunch of kids go on vacation.

They wanted as many of the "Others" as possible on South Field. It didn't matter to them who was caught in the crossfire. They wanted cold hard hits.

Maggie hated this strategy and wanted to battle that night, not with water balloons, but with her fists. Bode and Big Jessie once again calmed her down and told her to be patient.

The lone oak tree near the Divide always had a rope attached that was used to climb up to the lowest branches of the tree. However, that rope was in plain sight of everybody. The west would need to climb the oak from the side facing the north. That night, when he knew he wouldn't be seen, Bode snuck out to the oak and nailed two by four boards up the north face of the tree. His team could climb up that side without being seen.

CHAPTER 20
"THINGS OF THIS NATURE"

"Hey, Jared, I wanna talk to you," Jared's mom, Abigail called after him as he was about to go into the kitchen.

"What is it Mom? I got a game at two," Jared answered.

"I just want to chat for a second" she waved him into the living room.

Abigail Hanson was a skinny, wiry woman with more energy than most kids. She was very heavily involved with Jared and Missy's schools and was president of the middle school's Parent Teacher Organization. She ran the PTO with extreme efficiency. Being involved with school, she knew a lot of things about the kids. She was certainly aware of the rivalry between East and West Estates and especially, the rift between Jared and Bode. Mrs. Hanson and Bode's mom, Faith, not only served on the PTO, they were also good friends who knew each other well.

Their boys came up in their conversations often. If it was Jared and Blake who pelted each other, she would have never approached the subject. However, since the attack was against the west, and Bode was involved, she sensed that there was more to it than good, clean fun.

Jared sat down by his mom on the couch, a little apprehensive about the tone in her voice. He sensed what the conversation was going to be about.

"I heard that you guys had a little water balloon fight with some kids from West Estates" she began.

"Yeah, so what"? he questioned and shrugged his shoulders.

"Was it all in fun," as she looked him straight in the eye with the classic mom look.

"Sure......uhh, yeah, just water balloons," he shrugged again.

"I heard Timothy Lyle got hurt pretty bad, kinda rough play for a fifth grader don't........."

It was now clear in Jared's mind, Missy had squealed on him. "See Mom, that's your problem," Jared cut her off "you believe everything Missy tells you. She's only in fourth grade too and that......."

"Missy didn't tell me anything," it was her turn to cut him off this time, her voice raised, "You don't think that I talk to other parents, that I live in a vacuum?" her voice raised even higher.

Jared shrugged again with a disgusted, faraway look on his face.

Mrs. Hanson continued "I guess he got banged up pretty good. You know anything about that?"

"No," he lied.

"Who's idea was it to go over there and attack them?"

"I don't know, we just all thought it up and did it," he lied again as he looked at her with a blank look on his face.

"Just all got up and went over there, no planning or anything huh?" She was more insistent.

"Ya…..pretty much," he lied a third time.

"From what I understand enough water hit the ground to make home base a mud hole."

"People love to exaggerate," Jared rolled his eyes.

"Did you hit Bode with a water balloon?" Her questioning became more pointed.

"I might have, I hit a lot of people," his lies were starting to become more complex.

"Was he your main target, Jared?" as her eyes met his, an annoyed look came over his face.

"It was just a stupid water balloon fight, it doesn't mean anything, Mom," the way he drug out the word 'Mom' infuriated her.

"Look", Mrs. Hanson almost yelled, "I know you two don't like each other."

Jared looked away, not saying anything. She sensed she was starting to get really loud so she took a deep breath and calmed herself down.

"I bet a lot of the kids went over there to have some fun. However, I think your motives were deeper than a harmless water balloon fight," she continued.

"That's all it was, Mom, just a water balloon fight," he replied in a sing-song manner.

She calmed down even further, "Jared, situations like this can end very badly. I want you to calm it down and stay away from Bode. In fact, you're not allowed over in West Estates at all until I say so and you get this out of your system, got it?"

"It's all good, Mom," he replied.

"Alright, dinner is at 6:30, so be back here at about six with Missy." She motioned that he could go. As he was on his way out the door, she stopped him once more.

"By the way Jared," she said with a smile "never ever play poker or start a life of crime."

"What," he said perturbed.

"Your lower lip twitches when you lie, you are no good at it." The smile on her face was as triumphant as it was wide. Jared rolled his eyes, waved his hand as if to blow her off, and walked out the door.

CHAPTER 11
A CALM, PEACEFUL DAY

Thursday turned out to be a hot day, overcast and still. Bode thought this was a good thing as the balloons would have no wind resistance. He and the rest of the West waited in the Pit while Shaun and another boy passed the ball back and forth near the divide. They were to call when the others gathered for their daily pickup game of soccer. It was a gamble. The West couldn't be sure if Jared and the "Others" were going to play that day or not. They didn't have long to wait. At about 2:00, Shaun called Steven to announce the first of the "Others" had arrived on the soccer field and were putting on their shin guards and cleats.

"Good job, let us know when more arrive. We want as many as possible," Steven said and relayed the news to the rest of the West.

"Tell them to keep throwing ball like everything is normal," Bode commanded.

It didn't take long for the boys to call back and report that many more others had arrived at South Field. Steven asked for a list of names.

"I don't know," Shaun retorted, "I don't know most of them, they're not in my class."

Steven asked him to count them and his reply was about thirteen or so. "That's good, let's move out, its showtime!" Bode said.

Then there was the problem of Cree, Brook and Missy, who were camped out as usual on the playground. The girls actions, if they were to shout, wave or point, could give away the west's sneak attack. The answer was simple; collect enough money to send them to Boerner's Stop 'N' Go Carry-Out for ice cream. As the others gathered on South field to play soccer, Big Jessie casually walked over to them.

"Mom gave me some money for you to get some ice cream," Big Jessie held out a heap of change and crumpled $1 bills.

"Why?" asked Cree.

"Yummm!" said Brook and Missy.

"Do you want ice cream or not?" Big Jessie said, annoyed.

"Ya!" they said in unison.

"Then take this and go over to Boerner's and get some," Big Jessie said, his voice slightly raised.

"Last one there is a rotten egg!" yelled Missy and the three were off across North field to the far bridge and past the East kids who just starting to assemble to play soccer on south field.

When they got to Boerner's Stop 'N' Go, Jim Boerner was working the counter. This delighted the girls. The girls knew his scoops of ice cream were always bigger. He usually gave them an extra scoop at no extra cost as long as his parents weren't in the store and watching. This time was no different. For Cree, it was Neapolitan and strawberry crème; Brook, Butter Pecan and chocolate and for Missy, it was two big scoops of Mint Chocolate Chip all the way. The girls thanked Jim and paid him, even though they were fifty two cents short, and left. They settled down on the bench outside of the store and gorged on ice cream, oblivious to the battle that was about to begin on Boerner's field behind the strip mall.

Blake noticed the two boys throwing ball in North Field and didn't think anything about it. In his eyes, and most of the others, they had won. A couple of kids still brought wave blaster and sat them by the bleachers, but for the most part, the others were off high alert.

Jared walked up to him and they both looked toward North Field

Blake muttered "we won," with a smile on his face.

"We sure did," Jared said with a huge smile, his hand on Blake's shoulder.

CHAPTER 22
STRIKE FORCE

Three figures ran along the Divide, weapons on their backs, hair flying behind them, concealed by the vegetation that grew there. The sunlight mixed with the shadows of the shrubbery made them look like stealthy assassins. Their movements were precise and with a purpose as they moved through the brush jumping over bushes and dodging branches as they ran. Samantha was in the lead with Julie and Leslie behind her, Julie and Leslie were the two girls that Samantha and Sara mistook for the Shaw girls when they attacked with the water balloons. They crept through the bushes and shrubs along the divide making sure they weren't seen, creeping along and pausing every so often to make sure no one was looking. Bode led his group out of the far path, along Boerner's field, to the divide. Nothing was amiss. The two boys still passed the ball like nothing was going on and all was quiet. Across the divide, the East's soccer game was in full swing. "Other's" were sitting on the small set of bleachers, their backs to their attackers.

They crawled out of the brush by the oak, crouching down, moving ever so slowly. None of the "Others" were even looking their way. Across North Field to their right, they could make out the rest of the squad, creeping along the edge of Boerner's Farm field. One by one, the girls climbed the make shift-ladder of 2x4's nailed into the oak tree and took their positions on the lower branches. From their vantage point, they could watch the positioning of the rest of the West and watch the attack unfold. Bode, Big Jessie and Maggie crept along the edge of Boerner's field, keeping ever so low in the grass and making sure no one across the Divide could spot them. The tall bushes that grew along the Divide were enough to hide them if they kept low.

They got to the Divide and spread out, taking their positions along the creek. Steven, Mark, Timmy and a couple of other kids followed and spread out along the edge of the Divide. The boys quit throwing ball and crouched down to join them, looking first to make sure none of the "Others" were paying attention.

The army was set for their assault.

"I need to find a way to warn her," David thought as he looked out of his bedroom window in anticipation of the West's attack. He could see the others gathering to play soccer. Like clockwork, Kelsey sat down on the bleachers and started writing in her notebook.

"Well", he thought, "I don't have her number and I ain't about to go talk to her," he thought. He didn't even have the nerve to even say hi let alone talk to her.

"Oh well, it's too late now anyway," he said aloud as he looked toward north field and could see the West creeping along the edge of his family's farm field, all with weapons.

Not missing a beat, David grabbed a lawn chair, an old hollow metal sweeper attachment that he had saved, and some of his older brother's fireworks.

CHAPTER 23
THE WEST COUNTERATTACKS

Timmy crawled over by Bode and awaited his signal. None of the "Others" suspected a thing. Bode waited to give the signal to fire at will. He wanted to wait for a penalty call in the game so that most of them would be on one side of the field. He didn't have to wait long. Sneak illegally slide-tackled Joy and she hit the ground with a thud. Maci blew her whistle and it was time for a penalty kick. With almost everyone down at one goal, the time had come.

David set his lawn chair on the edge of the field among the soybeans. He then rammed the sweeper attachment into the ground so it would stand on its own. Taking various Roman Candles and bottle rockets, he tied the wicks together with a small piece of string and stuck them in the metal tube with the wicks sticking out of the end. He was ready. If the West were going to attack, he was going to provide the sights and sounds of war! A few others looked him but paid no attention to him.

His odd behavior was so common place that few even paid any attention to him anymore. David knew this and used it to his advantage, although it secretly hurt his feelings.

A ball was kicked out of bounds near David and a girl went to retrieve it. She looked at him with a quizzical glance. He smiled and waved as if it was normal to be sitting in a soybean field in a lawn chair with fireworks.

Big Jessie whispered to Bode "What is Dorkboy doing?"

"It doesn't matter, we can't turn back now," Bode replied.

And with that, Bode tapped Timmy on the head and Timmy pulled the trigger on his makeshift water balloon launcher. The balloon sailed effortlessly over the divide and landed near the bleachers in a nice pink splat. Bode, Big Jessie and Steven unloaded. Then everyone fired at once.

One balloon hit mid soccer field, another hit a kid in the chest and the one hit Greg on the ground near his leg, pink splatter everywhere. Several others were hit next, pink staining their soccer jerseys.

Half of the "Others" quit playing, dazed at what was happening, the rest of the team were not aware. Lexi and Maci were pelted from behind, pink water spraying and dying their hair.

Kelsey was hit next, smacked from behind as she sat on the bleachers.

"Not again!" she said aloud. The blast actually hurt as it smacked the back of her head.

The West was an affective attacking force, cocking and firing their launchers. The balloons met their mark to various degrees. The onslaught was never ending. Between the steady streams of pink water from Wave blasters and the multiple balloons launched or thrown, the "Others" were already in total disarray.

When Timmy fired the first shot, David lit the wicks. The Roman candles and bottle rockets flew up and exploded, making a colorful display in the air mixed with the loud bang that came with it. David let out a loud long YEEEEEHAAAAA!!

The fireworks exploding in the air, mixed with the pink water spattering on the ground and the kids made for an impressive sight. The reports from the fireworks only added to the confusion on the field. The soccer field started to look like a pink abstract painting, as if a giant paintbrush came down from the sky and starting flicking pink paint.

Jared and Blake now realized the attack unfolding and started to run toward the bridge. Greg turned to North Field only to get hit full in the face. Joy was smacked in the back of her white jersey, turning it a light pink.

Lexi had been showing off her new Columbus Crew jersey, which was now splattered with pink spots. Maci's blond hair was streaked with pink where a wave blaster got her. Jared yelled and pointed toward North field as the West all fired again. Two balloons hit Sneak in the back of his legs as he tried to run away from the attack. Several others were now pelted. The pink dye mixed with sweat ran down their arms.

A group of kids joined Jared and Blake as they ran toward the bridge. Some grabbed their Wave blasters while others didn't care, and were done playing with water. They were going to end this now. This was Julie, Leslie and Samantha's cue to strike. They didn't jump out of the tree; they just dropped, fell to one knee, pulled the wave blasters strapped to their backs and fired. The blasts were strong enough to hold them off, giving Bode, Big Jessie and Timmy time to reach the bridge, water balloon launchers loaded.

Big Jessie fired first, missing Jared's face. Timmy's blast hit Blake full in the stomach. He reeled back from the force of the blast breathless, landed on his butt and fell off the bridge into the Divide, hitting his head on the bridge as he fell.

The girls were still providing a steady stream of water from the wave blasters, making it hard for everyone to see. The entire attack force was there at that point; their balloons meeting their mark on the counterattack, making them all reel back. By this time more of the East started running toward the bridge. The steady firepower that the West administered on the "Others" as they got near the bridge did not stop. Splat after relentless splat of pink water prevented any further advance. Blake now pulled himself out of the shallow water of the Divide, a huge welt on his head. In confusion, he looked up toward North Field only to get smacked in the shoulder with yet another balloon, adding insult to injury.

And just like that, Bode gave the signal to fall back and the entire West retreated across North Field. The attack was fast, hard and relentless.

Jared and Greg started to follow but the West was already headed up the far path to the safety of the pit. In a weird twist of karma, it was now the East that saw only butts and elbows.

The results were staggering. The "Others" thought that their attack could not be outdone. They were wrong. The west hit twice as fast, twice as hard and left twice the mark. The soccer field was a pink, splattered mess.

Lexi, angry that her new jersey was ruined, was yelling up a storm. Blake was okay even though he hit his head when he tumbled into the divide. He started to groan from the pain. Jared heard his best friend below the bridge in the Divide.

"Blake, you OK?" Jared exclaimed out of concern. He and a couple of kids helped Blake out of the Divide, the welt on his head getting bigger and bigger.

Jared looked toward North Field and the west half of the subdivision. There was no sound, no celebration, no yelling. The only sign of life were Cree, Brook and Missy walking back from Boerner's, talking among themselves, not even noticing the pink stains on the soccer fields, bleacher and most of the East.

Everyone looked at each other. Almost all had some kind of pink on them. Lexi's new jersey was ruined. Maci's blonde hair had pink streaks in it, the back of Kelsey's head was completely pink. Jared and Blake were almost completely covered, pink in Jared's curly hair, Joy's back was covered, and her legs were light pink. Greg had pink splotches all over him. Not much was said except for Joy and Kelsey as they marched passed Jared.

"Great job jerk; Thanks a lot" Joy said through gritted teeth.

"For once I'm inclined to agree with her," Kelsey said in her quick delivery. Jared, who was speechless, looked at them as well as everyone else, defeat and frustration in his eyes.

"Actually this could be a good look for me," Maci said, admiring the pink streaks in her hair, making use of the reflection on the screen of her cell phone.

The East thought they had won. They didn't think that their attack could be outdone. They were wrong. The West hit twice as fast, twice as hard, and twice as effective including the pink dye which, as it was discovered, did not wash off easily.

CHAPTER 24
"I SEE MORE FROM THIS FIELD
THAN YOU WILL EVER KNOW"

Jared saw David, who was packing up his chair and his metal tube and ran over to him as David started to walk toward his house.

"You know about this all along, didn't you?" Jared demanded.

David stopped and turned around, and replied with a smirk, "I heard something about it."

"You could have told me or yelled, said something," Jared persisted.

"Like what, you wanted this war, didn't you?" David was adamant.

"That's cool," Jared said sarcastically, "guess we know what side you're on."

"I don't choose sides," David responded, "I just wanted to watch the fun and games!"

"You know David, I've always defended you," Jared countered, the pink dye dripping off of his face and arms, "I thought maybe you would try to let us know about this instead of egging them on. I thought we were friends……"

"Oh, because I let you copy my math homework on the bus. That's some friendship." David cut him off, the coldness dripping from his words. He stared Jared right in the face.

Jared was getting mad, his fists started to clinch. David dropped the chair and metal tube and faced him. Jared suddenly knew to let it go. Although he was a weirdo to most of the kids, Jared knew one thing about David Boerner. He was not a wimp. David was a farm boy with three older brothers. He was agile, strong and knew how to fight. He also had a lot of upper body strength because of all of the chores he did around the family farm.

Jared slowly turned to leave and David piped up, "Hey, if you want to know what the West is up to, send your boy Darin to spy on them in the pit. He did a killer job of imitating me!" he said in disgust.

Jared could say nothing at this point; he knew he was defeated all around. They looked at each other for a second when David broke the silence.

"I have seen more from this field than you will ever know," he said adamantly. With that, he picked up his stuff and walked through the soybeans back to his house.

That night phone calls began to fly and e-mails sent as kids from East Estates came home painted pink. All across Buckeye Estates, many kids were grounded.

CHAPTER 25
THE STRAW AND THE CAMEL'S BACK

The day started out perfect; perfect weather, perfect temperature, and perfect sunshine. In fact, it was a perfect day for any outdoor sport. Most of the kids from both sides at this point were ungrounded. All was peaceful in both North and South fields.

It had been more than a week since the West's massive attack that left most of the East pink. Since the dye was hard to get off, many Others still had remnants of pink dye on their skin. Neither side had forgotten about the attack from just a week before, nor were they complacent about it. Neither side was finished with the war either, but there was a weird, uneasy unspoken cease fire for now.

Jared put on his shin guards and looked toward North field. The West was starting to get together and warm up for baseball. He had not forgotten, nor did he think it was harmless fun. He took it personally.

As usual, the West was playing baseball, the "Others" playing soccer.

Bode, on the other hand, was quite pleased with himself and his team. He now looked to South field with a smile on his face. In his mind, the West had won. They had proven that they could band together and hit harder, faster and stronger. If the "Others" wanted to try it again, they would be ready.

The baseball game on North Field started around 1:00 PM. Mark, one of the best batters, stepped up to the plate. Samantha was on the mound like normal. She knew he could hit anything. Big Jessie, behind the plate gave her a signal for a slider; she shook it off; a curve ball; she shook her head no; fastball; she nodded in agreement. She performed her wind up, the pitch was flawless. Mark took the bait and swoosh, strike one. Big Jessie threw the ball back.

Samantha waited for the signal. A knuckleball; she shook her head no, a curveball; she nodded. The windup, the pitch and the swing, Mark caught a piece of it sending it back into the backstop, foul tip. Big Jessie returned the ball.

Samantha waited for his signal. A change up; she shook it off; a slider, no, she knew he could hit it; a fast ball, yes, that was the pitch she wanted. The wind up, pitch and Mark swung at the ball with all his might, keeping his eye on it the whole time. CRAAACK! He nailed it in the dead center of the bat.

The hit was a beauty; the baseball grew wings as it sailed over the infield, then over the outfield, over the divide and came down hard near the bleachers on south field, bounced once and hit Maci right in the thigh.

"OOOOWWWW," she screamed with all her might as she went down on one knee. She was so loud everyone stopped playing soccer and look over. Blake was the first to the baseball. He picked it up and hurled it back towards North Field over the divide while some helped Maci to her feet. That might have been the end of it but in Jared's mind, it was on purpose.

There is an expression, "the straw that broke the camel's back" meaning one event could spark a larger event and trigger a course of action. That baseball made Jared snap. He quickly walked off the field, over the bridge and onto North field, followed by everyone else. His eyes were on fire.

"C'mon Jared, calm down," Sneak said.

"Just relax, it was an accident," someone else chimed in.

"Man, we just got out of trouble, don't do this," Greg said as he tried to put his hand on Jared's shoulder, but he pulled away with a tug. The West saw the whole group quickly walking towards them and assembled to walk out to stop them, Bode in the lead. Bode knew what this meant, and the anger and fear reverberated through his entire body, the same for Jared. There was a time when the balloon fights, the rivalry, the general dislike and distrust was kind of fun. It was almost exciting. But now, the fun was over as the situation suddenly became serious.

Bode and Jared slowly came toward each other, fists clinched. The girls from the east and west faced each other in a line and the insults started to fly. Maggie and Kelsey were the first start the jawing, hurling verbal abuse at each other's head. Lexi and Maci started in on Leslie and Julie and they fired back, slam after verbal slam.

"Water balloons weren't enough, now you're gonna use baseballs?" Blake yelled at Bode and Big Jessie, who said nothing. Bode was too busy staring at his arch rival, Jared, who was slowly walking toward him.

Cree was swinging on the swingset while Brook and Missy were busy fiddling with Missy's MP3 player and speakers when she noticed the crowd of people assembling on the edge of the baseball field near the divide. She didn't see any water balloons or wave blasters anywhere. She sensed that the way the kids were acting, something was wrong.

"Hey! hey, you guys, look," she said pointing toward the group of kids. Brook and Missy followed her gaze and pointed finger to the huge mass of kids now assembled.

"What's going on?" Missy said aloud as Cree stopped swinging. All three were now looking.

"I don't know, but it looks bad!" Cree said with caution in her voice, "let's go see what's up."

The three girls stopped what they were doing and wandered over to the group, a little curious, kind of anxious and a little scared.

Rosie and Joy, best friends, now faced each other, not realizing how ugly the situation was becoming.

"Okay, ummm, we can't stand each other, right? That's how were "supposed" to act," as Joy air quoted "supposed" and said it with emphasis.

"Oh, yeah, that's right," replied Rosie, "okay, I'll go first. Ummm, I don't approve of your kind and you smell bad."

"Good one!" Joy laughed, "ummmm, let's see, your hair's a rat's nest and your breath is real nasty."

"My breath's not nasty, smelly girl!" Rosie replied, "speaking of which, check out this new gum."

"Oh, cool, blueberry cream," as Joy took a piece and the two started to giggle at how absurd they sounded.

Meanwhile, Maggie and Kelsey kept firing verbal abuse at each other. Lexi and Maci were yelling at Samantha and Sara who were starting to yell too when Big Jessie stepped in.

"Girls, Hey girls!" He tried to say without shouting. They were not listening.

"GIRLS!!" he shouted at the top of his lungs. They all stopped and looked at him.

"SHUT UP!!" Jessie was now yelling quite loudly. This didn't sit well as every girl that was yelling now turned to him with one foot off to the side, hands on their hips and looking pretty perturbed that he would shout an order at them.

"So, you wanna hit us with baseballs?" Jared yelled at Bode.

"So, you got your little sister to steal my ball glove?" Bode retorted.

Brook, Cree and Missy were now standing at the edge of the group. They were confused as to what was going on. In their minds, it was harmless water balloon battles, but they didn't understand it was much deeper than that.

"No, no, no," Brook tried to explain.

"I did not!" Missy protested.

The group, both east and west, was now turned toward Bode and Jared. They had everyone's full attention.

"You and your little followers started this whole thing by attacking us with water balloons!" Jared belted out.

"That's crap!" Bode replied, "it was you who attacked us first!"

"Oh, yeah? Who attacked Joy and Kelsey for no reason?" Jared's face was now on fire, his cheeks read with anger. Samantha and Sara gulped.

"It wasn't that bad," Joy protested but her voice could not be heard over the din.

David was cleaning off his boots after his chores when he heard the commotion. He stopped what he was doing and came to the edge of the field to watch. He was not in the least bit surprised that this would happen, but he wasn't pleased about it. He watched this feud from the outside looking in for years now and still didn't see or understand why a rivalry existed at all.

"Well, who thought it was a good idea to hit Timmy with a brick?" Bode shouted back. It was Lexi and Maci's turn to gulp.

"It wasn't a brick," Lexi protested but nobody was listening. All the time Bode and Jared were shouting, they were moving closer and closer to each other with their fists clenched. They were quickly reaching the point of no return. The prejudice, the fear, anxiety and anger were coming to a head. All the years of being told or taught by older siblings or common knowledge that the other side was the enemy was coming to its fruition.

Jared snapped. He jumped at Bode trying to push him down or knock him off balance. Bode moved back from the force of the push but stayed upright, his strong thick frame helping him. The two began to wrestle standing up as shouts began from the group.

"Hit'em!" Steven shouted.

"C'mon Jared, kick him!" yelled Blake.

"Take him down!" Big Jessie belted out.

"Hit him in the face!" Greg coached.

"STOOOOP!" cried Missy.

The two were trading punches now. Jared had Bode in a headlock as Bode repeatedly hit Jared in the ribs. Just like that, they were on the ground. Bode on top at first, then Jared. The two continued to trade punches on the ground amongst the shouts and protests from the kids gathered around. Now Jared had Bode's left arm pinned and Bode was kicking Jared in the thigh. Bode got his arm free in time to crack Jared in the temple. Jared reacted with a swing which connected to Bode's arm. Blood was starting to flow from cuts on both of them.

The shouts of the crowd were deafening now as kids from both sides were cheering them on.

"Own this, kick him," someone shouted.

"You got this" another kid yelled.

Somehow, the two briefly managed to separate and they were back on their feet. They stopped for a quick second. All of the power each one had was transferred to the right fists.

Like two rams about to butt heads, they lunged at each other as they threw their punches at the same time with all their might. Both punches met their mark with a sickening crack; Bode hit Jared square on the nose, Jared found his mark on Bode's left cheek. Blood flew from Jared' nose and splattered on Bode's fist, droplets of blood suspended in the air. The crowd gasped, Jared reeled back from the blow, spun around and fell down, landing on his butt past Bode. Bode reeled back, staggered past Jared and went down on one knee, holding his face in his hands. The blow left him dizzy as he tried to regain his equal librium. Jared got up quickly, paused and sat back down, blood now streaming down his chin and onto his shirt. The fight lasted about a minute but for the two involved as well as the crowd, it seemed like it lasted for hours. Jared was now on one knee, holding his hand to his nose trying to stop the bleeding. Bode was bent over, holding his cheek and eye, still dizzy, he staggered a bit. Most of the spectators rushed to the side of their respective friend trying to assess the seriousness of the injuries.

"So why did you guys start this war, Bode?" Jared said between gasps, still on one knee. "why Joy and Kelsey, they didn't do anything to you."

Before Bode could answer, Samantha piped up, "Me and Sara hit them with the balloons. We thought they were Julie and Leslie from the back," she continued finally coming clean. Julie and Leslie shot each other a confused look.

"It was supposed to be just a joke," Samantha admitted. "We're sorry." Sara nodded in agreement.

"Okay, then," Bode started, "then why did your little sister steal my ball glove?" he said, glaring right at Jared.

"What?" Missy protested, "I didn't steal anything." She was crying now.

"And why did you write crap about me on Boerner's wall," Blake said looking right at Mark.

"I didn't write anything," Mark shouted.

"You idiot, your ball glove is right here!" Brook yelled as she held up Bode's glove. "It's been in plain sight in the garage for the last two weeks. You're just too stupid to even look for it. You just wanted to blame someone for your mistake."

"Whaaaaa?" Bode stammered.

"I picked it up where you left it after a game!" Brook said through clenched teeth.

The truth sunk in deep for Bode, and it stung more than Jared's punch. He looked over at his little sister, regret showed on his face. It also became very clear to Mark as he looked at Missy's brown MP3 player case in her hand that it was not a ball glove. Bode looked over at him for an explanation. He knew Bode wanted an answer. Without waiting to be asked, Mark gestured at Missy.

"Well.....it....looked like a glove from a distance."

"Who hit my little brother with a rock?" Maggie demanded, looking at the entire East in the eye.

"It was a balloon!" Lexi spoke up, tears in her eyes, "I really didn't mean to throw it that hard, honest, I felt so bad, sorry." She meant it. Although Maggie and Timmy glared at her, they could tell she was truly sorry.

"Just everyone quit fighting," Missy said meekly, tears streaming down her face.

"That's gotta be broken," Maci said, moving Jared hand away from his nose.

"C'mon," Greg said helping him up, "let's get you home." Jared got up slowly, still wobbly.

"Okay, it's over, you guys shake," Big Jessie commanded.

"Jessie's right, shake hands," Blake agreed.

Jared and Bode looked at each other for a brief second. Jared started to walk towards him, hand partially extended. Bode, however turned and started to walk away amongst the protests of everyone else there.

"C'mon Bode," Julie yelled.

"It's the thing to do," Steven said.

"It's over man, shake and let it go," insisted Mark. Jared said nothing. He just put his hand back over his nose and turned to walk home.

"Bode, c'mon man," Big Jessie put his hand on Bode's shoulder. Bode shrugged it off.

A voice came from the edge of the field,

"No, you won't regret this or nothing. You won't think about this decision for years to come or nothing!"

It was David, sarcasm prominent in his every word. He had watched the entire thing. Although he enjoyed watching the water balloon fights, he, like everyone else there, knew that the fun was over. Now everyone saw David in a different light. He was not joking or acting goofy anymore. Arms outstretched, disgusted look on this face, David was serious. Bode shot him a dirty look and kept walking slowly home.

"Home," he thought, "just through the far path, to Semicircle, up Semicircle to Estates Way. Mom is home today and she would know what to do about my eye and cheek." He thought to himself.

"Mom," he thought.

Suddenly her words came flooding back to him. He could hear her speaking to him. He could hear her speaking plain as day in her soft Kentucky accent.

"A writer of some ability once wrote something to the effect of 'when you go out in search of monsters, don't become one yourself.'" This made Bode stop in his tracks, most of the crowd looking after him. Although he didn't want to admit it, he was becoming the monster. However, his foolish pride made him keep on walking home.

No one said a thing, the air was quiet and still. Some simply nodded, most kids turned toward home. It was over, Cortney and Joy stood there quietly, still amazed at what happened. Missy said a tearful goodbye to Cree and Brook and followed her big brother home. David watched everyone leave.

CHAPTER 26
TO THE EMERGENCY ROOM

Two cars from Buckeye Estates raced from different locations towards Broad Street, headed for the emergency room at Prairie Woods Methodist Hospital. It was the closest. Bode and his mom got there first and sat in the waiting room as Jared and his mom walked in. Bode and Jared's eyes met. They looked at each other briefly, but said nothing as Jared took a seat on the other side of the waiting room.

"Fancy meeting you here," Faith Catron said.

"Yeah, really," Jared's mom replied dryly.

After what seemed like an eternity to the two mothers, the doctors finally came out separately to address the injuries. The tally was pretty staggering for a middle grade fist fight. Bode; black eye, fractured cheek bone, cuts on his cheek and hands and a broken knuckle. Jared; broken nose, various cuts, broken hand and bruised ribs.

CHAPTER 27
THE LONE OAK BY THE DIVIDE

Bode was the first to call. He called Jared. The conversation was short but to the point. The first e-mails were initiated by Big Jessie. It was addressed to whoever was allowed to have an e-mail account. His main focus was Jared and Blake, but, if he copied everyone, he thought it might generate even more interest. Soon, phone calls and e-mails started flying, conversations went on and soon everyone knew. The meeting was set for the coming Saturday. All that could make it were to meet at the lone oak tree by the divide in North field at 1:00 PM. There was a meeting to be held.

That Saturday, kids from both east and west met at the oak tree. They were tired and cautious. The West stayed on their side of the oak, the "Others" stayed in a group near the bridge across the divide. There were muffled conversations, but, for the most part the crowd was pretty quiet. The air was hot with a slight breeze.

Jared and Bode approached the oak followed by both groups. They both looked like zombies; Jared, with a bandage on his nose and cast on part of his hand and arm and Bode with a bandage on his cheek, his hand in a cast as well.

Neither one said a word. Steven got to work stripping the bark off a portion of the oak at about eye level while Bode and Jared got out their pocket knives. When Steven was finished, Bode started to carve .When he was done, Jared finished what Bode had started. Both groups looked on quietly. Jared was done with his part and Steven stepped forward to blow off the wood shavings. Everyone stepped back to ponder for a second what had been carved. The Playground Three looked at the carving, smiled and skipped off towards the swing sets, and way off in the distance, David stood there at the edge of his field, silently watching.

An agreement had been suggested and all the kids from both sides agreed. A ceasefire needed to be made. An agreement not drawn up on paper, written in blood or etched in stone, but, with one word carved in the wood of the lone oak tree which had stood their silently for so many years.

It read "TRUCE".

Bode and Jared looked at each other again in total silence, their faces solemn. They did not shake hands, smile or act friendly toward each other. They were not friends and did not try to be. Like all the kids in Buckeye Estates, there was a mutual respect for each other. Both sides looked at the word for a minute or two and slowly, silently, they all walked away in different directions.

CHAPTER 28
A DIFFERENT KIND OF WAR

Things calmed down and returned to normal. The east still played soccer and for the most part kept to South Field. The west played baseball and hung out in North Field. There was still a wariness each side had toward the other, but the general feeling was that the war was over. Nobody expected that a different kind of war was about to begin.

One day, about three weeks after Bode's and Jared's fight, a strange thing happened. Something no one from the East expected. The Others were out playing soccer, some kids were watching or talking and Kelsey was on the bleachers writing in her journal as always. Jared was sitting on the bleachers as well. He had to take a break from sports to let his broken nose and fingers heal, and the bandage on his nose didn't let him breathe very well. He was not happy about it. Maci and Lexi were reffing, and about to blow the whistle ending the first quarter.

Big Jessie and Maggie suddenly appeared at the edge of the soccer field. It seemed as though they were waiting for something. Big Jessie picked up an extra soccer ball at the edge of the field and was casually throwing it into the air. Greg was the first to notice them after the whistle blew, ending the first quarter.

"What's up? You need something?" Greg asked the pair.

"Ya," Big Jessie replied with the soccer ball in his hands, a big smile on his face. At first it seemed like he wasn't going to give the ball back.

Jared stood up and started walking toward them.

"Oh no, here we go again," Blake said under his breath.

"We wanna challenge you to a game of baseball," Big Jessie said with conviction.

"Baseball?" Blake replied.

"Yeah, ya know, you take a bat and hit a little white ball and someone with a big ball glove tries to catch it," Maggie was more than factious.

"We get the picture," Blake said, "but we play soccer, we don't ...."

"You're on!" Jared cut him off, his voice still nasally from the broken nose.

"Cool, meet us at North Field in one hour, you gotta have at least nine or you forfeit," Big Jessie said with authority, a big smile on his face.

Maggie now looked directly at Kelsey sitting on the top tier of the bleachers.

"You could play too, princess, but we wouldn't want you to ding up those perfectly painted fingernails," Maggie was smirking. Kelsey fumed.

"Be there, one hour," Big Jessie said as he threw the ball to Jared. With that, the two retreated across the divide.

When they were out of earshot, Blake looked at Jared, "You're on?" he questioned Jared's response.

"Sure, why not?" Jared replied with a smile.

"Easy for you to say since you ain't gonna play," Greg replied annoyed. Jared shrugged off the comment.

"Ummmmmm...........okaaaaaay. I got a glove," Blake replied.

"I'll play, but they're gonna hand our butts to us," someone said, "You know that's right, don't you" looking at Jared.

"I'm in," said Greg.

"Me too" his brothers chimed in.

Jared looked around for other volunteers. He knew that most had ball gloves and a bat or at least access to them.

"Let's beat 'em at their own game," a sneer came across Greg face.

"Don't you think that's what their thinking, humiliate us in another way," Lexi chimed in.

"Here's what's gonna happen people, were gonna go over there, get surrounded and they are gonna jack us on their turf," the ever paranoid Sneak blurted out. "You can forget me, no way"

Greg, always ready to keep Sneak in check, grabbed his shoulders from behind.

"You're playing whether you like it or not" he said with a huge smile.

"Don't man handle me, dude," Sneak pulled away as Greg smiled some more. "Alright I'll play", Sneak shouted "but you owe me a thing of Ho-Hos for this, and I'm playing left field". Sneak picked this position simply because left field was closest to a bridge across the Divide, and an escape route.

"I'll play," a couple more kids volunteered, making the count to eight players.

"Joy, what about you?" Jared asked.

"Ummm, I'm a 'soccer player'," Joy said with a snotty tone to her voice, air quoting soccer player.

"Okay, that's eight, we need one more," Jared looked around for one more.

"Lexi, Maci, what about you two?" he asked.

"I don't think so," Lexi responded.

"No, thanks," Maci agreed.

Maci turned to Kelsey who was sitting on the top bleacher with a sour look on her face, still fuming at Maggie's comment.

"What about you, Kel, you're not going to let Maggie talked to you like that, are you?" Maci said with a devilish look on her face.

Kelsey thought about it for a second and slammed down her journal and pen, making the pen fly up in the air.

"How hard can it be?" A determined look came across her face as she shot up and walked down the bleachers. Maci smiled knowing she stirred Kelsey up.

"We better grab gloves and warm up," Blake suggested, "I'm sure were gonna be rusty".

The "Others" started to warm up on North field. As for Kelsey, well, it was harder than she thought. Unlike her big sister, Kelsey was not very athletic. In fact, she was about as athletic as a tree sloth.

Blake threw her a grounder which smacked her in her shin. He then threw her a pop-up and she completely overplayed it, the ball barely missing her ear. He tried a very lightly-thrown line drive and she turned her face away, glove and arm extended in defense.

"Yaaawwoo!" she cried "you don't have to beam it at me" she shouted, her words very fast and defiant.

While this was happening, Maggie and Timmy were watching from across the field.

"Oh man, she's horrible!" Maggie said to her little brother, a disgusted look on her face, "This is pathetic!" Maggie was so annoyed she couldn't even gloat about her arch rival's shortcomings with baseball.

Kelsey next tried batting. Her first two swings were awkward, sluggish and nowhere near the ball. The third pitch, thrown a little on the inside, caught one of her fingers.

"OOWW, that stings!" Kelsey yelled. With that, she threw down the bat and started walking towards the bench. The whole time she was yelling at the top of her lungs in her trademark rapid fire manner.

"This stupid game is dangerous. I quit, I'm not gonna get myself killed! I'm not going to the hospital for a dumb game, no way, forget it, not me, uh uh, no way, I'm done, stick a fork in me!" She yelled it so fast it was hard to understand her.

"You gotta play or we have to forfeit," Blake said as he followed her.

"Nope" was all she would blurt out.

"C'mon Lexi , you and Maci play," Blake pleaded. They shook their heads in unison.

Jared thought quickly, "Can we borrow one of you guys?" he said to the growing crowd on the other side of the field. They all shook their heads no.

"C'mon give her a break, give 'em all a break, they are new to this," came a voice from far across the field. This made Kelsey stop in her tracks. She twirled around, ran past Blake, picked up her borrowed ball glove and ran to the edge of Boerner's Farm Field.

"Hey, Dorkboy!" she called not really knowing where he was at. David was there as usual, lying amount the soybeans, baseball glove on his chest.

"Speaking," he replied in a high voice and held up his hand and waved. She spotted the waving hand and ran over to him. Without telling anyone her intentions or seeing if it was okay, she asked, "Wanna play some baseball?"

"I thought you'd never ask!" he replied as he stood up, patted the dirt off his butt and walked out of the soybean field.

"Okay, it's real easy, you just stand here and catch the ball and throw it back, I think," Kelsey instructed as David walked up to her.

"Your name is Kelsey?" David asked, ignoring her directions.

"Ummmm......... ya...." Kelsey looked at him with a puzzled look on her face.

"Yep, it's Kelsey................. Kelsey Lenore Shaw," David said very timidly, "it's ummmm very pretty................... just like you are." He could barely speak because he was so nervous.

Kelsey went from puzzled to flustered in a few short seconds and she started to blush. She turned partly away and looked at him out of the corner of her eye.

"Ummmmm.….Okay, uh, thanks," she stumbled and stammered all over her words, barely able to get them out of her mouth. This made David smile.

"Well, uhhhh……… you're gonna need this," she said as she held out the ball glove in her hand.

"I got my own," and held his up.

"Well okay, uh ………gotta go…………… ummmm have fun," she said and walked quickly across the field, looking over her shoulder a couple of times towards the bench where Joy, Cortney, Lexi and Maci gathered to watch the game.

David let out the biggest sigh of relief he had ever had. He did it. He finally got the nerve to talk to Kelsey. It took him almost a year but he did it. Something inspired him when she asked him to play and he threw shyness out of the window. Now he was on fire and ready to show everybody that he could play ball as well.

"This okay?" Jared yelled to the West.

"Ya, is everyone cool with me playing?" David shouted. The two questions were met with smirks and shrugs. Some were laughing that David was going to play baseball in cowboy boots!

"Sure," Bode said loudly with a huge smile on his face, "why not?"

When Kelsey got back to the bench, Joy couldn't help but to notice her flushed cheeks and weird grin.

"What's the matter with you?" Joy's question caught the attention of Rosie, Lexi and Maci. Kelsey half turned away, looking at them hesitantly out of the corner of her eye.

"I ….I think," she stammered, "ummm…Dorkboy….. just ummm…flirted with me."

"Whooohooo!" Lexi yelled, one fist in the air.

"Yeeaa, Kel!" Maci said clapping her hands. Joy and Cortney laughed.

The East batted first and it went three and out. When the east took the field, they put David in right field. Bode quickly huddled his team for some last minute instructions.

"You know what to do, anybody that can, hit it to right field."

"No problem," Steven piped up.

The West tried their best to hit everything they had at David, who fielded each ball with effortless ability. Fly balls, grounders, pop-ups were all snatched up with ease. Every ball he threw back to the infield was on target. If the play was at second base, he nailed it. If the play was at home, his throw was spot on.

The "Others" now had their turn at bat again, top of the third.

"Okay, so he can field, let's see if he can bat," Samantha said to herself atop the mound as David stepped up to the plate.

"This should be a quick out," Blake said dryly to no one in particular. Blake was wrong. The second pitch from Samantha was met with the end of David's bat, accompanied by the most beautiful "klunk" they had ever heard. The ball flew over the infield and the outfield with no sign of slowing down. The west kids watched it in despair.

David put the bat to his mouth like a microphone.

"Attention passengers, Flight 857 is cleared for takeoff," he said mustering his best official pilot's voice. The ball seemed to grow wings as it sailed over the divide and with several bounces, landed close to the back of the strip mall at Boerner's Corners.

David turned to Big Jessie behind the plate, chiding him "That was kinda far, did you think that was far, I don't know, what do you think, is that a home run?"

"Just run your bases," Big Jessie said, completely annoyed.

And run his bases he did in total Dorkboy fashion. He skipped toward first, twirled in the air and landed on the base; he stuck his arms out and "flew" to second base. Rounding second, he did a somersault followed by a dance to third base. At third base he patted his butt twice and sprinted to home plate, much to the chagrin of the West team. The East however, erupted in cheers and met him at home plate with high fives and pats on the back.

"This is a scam," Maggie yelled from centerfield, pointing at Kelsey, "you knew how good he was all along. Way to cheat Ugly in Pink!"

"PPPPPPFFFFFFFFFTTTTTTTTT,"
Kelsey responded with a raspberry.

The "Others" were right about losing the game. Despite David's efforts, who scored three of the runs, the east got crushed a whopping 11-4. The "Others" were at that point already contemplating a rematch. However, the next time would be on the soccer field, just to even the score.

THE END